THIS ISN'T OVER

ART OF PAYBACK
BOOK 3

DAN PETROSINI

COPYRIGHT

Print ISBN: 978-1-960286-78-9
Kindle ISBN: 978-1-960286-42-0
Printed in Naples, FL
1st Edition 2025
Library of Congress Control Number: 2025916609

<u>The Luca Mystery Series</u>

Am I the Killer

Vanished

The Serenity Murder

Third Chances

A Cold, Hard Case

Cop or Killer?

Silencing Salter

A Killer Missteps

Uncertain Stakes

The Grandpa Killer

Dangerous Revenge

Where Are They

Buried at the Lake

The Preserve Killer

No One is Safe

Murder, Money and Mayhem

The Golden Sellout

<u>Suspenseful Secrets</u>

Cory's Dilemma

Cory's Flight

Cory's Shift

<u>Art Of Payback</u>

Race To Revenge

Beyond Revenge

This Isn't Over

PART I

FOURTEEN YEARS EARLIER

Murder – transitive verb: to kill a person unlawfully and unjustifiably with premeditated malice.

1

"Nine-one-one, what's your emergency?"

Tyler Crane said, "My mother needs help!"

"What's happening with her?"

"She's on the floor and there's blood all over. I tried to get her up, but she won't get up."

"We're sending an ambulance and patrol cars."

"Hurry! Hurry!"

"Are you at 9943 Hunters Road?"

"Yes, it's our house. Hurry up!"

"Stay on the line with me. Are you in danger?"

"No. It's not me, it's my mom."

"I understand. Is anyone else there?"

"No. Nobody."

"What do you think happened?"

"Somebody stabbed her."

"Is she breathing?"

"No. I don't think so. Hurry, please."

"Try and calm down and I'll walk you through CPR."

"I don't know what to do."

"That's okay, I'll help you."

The dispatcher guided Tyler as he attempted to revive his mother.

Tyler said, "It's not working!"

"That's not unusual. Stay calm and let's do it again."

The dispatcher stayed with Tyler as he tried to get his mother to respond.

"She's not breathing! What should I do? Help me!"

"Are you sure you're doing the compressions properly?"

"I think so."

"Use both hands, center them on her chest. Make sure your elbows are locked and press down. Don't be afraid you're going to hurt her. We can fix that if you do. Her chest needs to compress by at least two inches."

"Two inches?"

"Yes. You need to do a lot of compressions, like a hundred a minute but make sure her chest returns to normal before doing the next one."

"I hear sirens, they're coming."

A Collier County Sheriff's patrol car screeched to a halt in front of the Livingston Estates home.

Tyler Crane ran to the front door, throwing it open. "In here!"

A uniformed officer jogged to the front door. "Is anyone besides your mother inside?"

"No, she's in the kitchen, on the floor."

"Stay outside until I call you."

Stepping into the house, Officer Goodwin put his hand on his holster. "Collier County Police!"

He walked through the family room into the kitchen. Next to the island lay a woman's body. Her yellow shirt was marred by several large blots of red.

Goodwin kneeled and checked her neck for a pulse. She

was cool to the touch. The officer guessed she had been dead for several hours.

"The ambulance is here!"

Goodwin got on his feet and went to the door.

Tyler said, "Is she going to be all right?"

Avoiding the kid's eyes, Goodwin said, "Let's wait and see what the medics say."

He directed the EMT techs to the kitchen as a dark sedan pulled up. Homicide Detective Mark Donovan got out of the unmarked car as another patrol car pulled up.

Goodwin approached Detective Donovan and filled him in. Donovan said, "Set up a perimeter. See if the boy has a father and get someone, a neighbor, anyone who can wait with the kid."

"He said he called his father but he's an hour away."

"Then check with a neighbor."

"I'll wait with the kid."

Donovan handed his car keys over. "Put the boy in my car. I need to see the crime scene before I talk to him."

He started for the house and turned around. "Put the kid in the car and move it onto the driveway."

Donovan disappeared inside. The detective paused at the entrance to the kitchen. Standing, two medics were talking. A bare foot was visible off the corner of the island.

Donovan said, "Is she deceased?"

They shook their heads, and the taller technician said, "She's been gone for a while."

"Okay. You can clear out."

As the EMT workers packed up, Donovan put booties and gloves on and stepped around the island. The body was sprawled, face down. She was braless, wearing a T-shirt and thin sweatpants. There appeared to be at least three separate sources of the pool of blood she lay in.

The detective pulled his cell out, phoning in a request for the medical examiner and a forensics unit. Pocketing the phone, he knelt by the body. He pulled a glove on and touched the woman's cheek with the back of his hand.

The skin was firm and cold, and the arms were covered with defensive knife wounds. She had struggled but had been overcome by her attacker. Donovan believed the assault was personal.

Donovan stood and surveyed the kitchen. The coffee maker looked unused. No mugs on the counter or in the sink. He opened the dishwasher. Two pieces of Tupperware and a couple of utensils were waiting to be cleaned.

He closed it and scanned the counter. A slot in the block holding knives was empty. Donovan pulled a knife out and examined it. Did the victim surprise an intruder who used the knife against her?

He gazed at the slider leading to a small, screened lanai. He walked around the kitchen table and tugged on the slider's handle. It rolled open. He stepped outside. A chaise lounge, a café table, and chairs framed the space.

Donovan approached the screen door, it was unlocked. A narrow stretch of grass was the only buffer before a wooded preserve. He circled around the home; there were no signs of forced entry.

Donovan walked to the edge of the property and peered into the woods. Had the killer entered or left this way? Vowing to check on where the home backed up to, he went back inside.

Camera slung over a shoulder, the department's photographer stepped into the kitchen. "How are you doing, Donovan?"

"I'd sure rather not be here."

"I hear you."

"Put booties on and don't disturb anything."

"You got it."

"The ME and forensics are on the way. I'm going outside to talk to the kid who found the victim."

Donovan scooted around the gurney the medics were rolling through the house. He went straight to a pocketbook on a table. He dug out the wallet and pulled out a driver's license. The victim was forty-two-year-old Ana Crane. He put it back and stepped outside.

A small crowd of onlookers had gathered at the perimeter of the isolated home. A van from WINK News was parked across the street.

Donovan kept his head down as he peeled off his gloves. He opened the door to his car, getting into the back seat next to Tyler Crane. Officer Goodwin got out of the car and Donovan said, "Hey, kiddo."

Tyler asked, "How's my mother?"

He searched for the right words. "They're working on her."

The kid pointed out the window. "But the ambulance people are leaving."

Donovan looked the kid in the eyes. He saw the lifeline of hope drifting away and put his hand on the boy's shoulder. "I'm sorry, buddy, but uh, your mom didn't make it."

Tyler's chin quivered. He ran the back of his hand across his upper lip and tears began to flow. Donovan rubbed the kid's back, and after a couple of minutes his sobbing ended.

Donovan said, "I'm really sorry, buddy. But now we have to be strong. We've got to catch the person who did this."

Tyler nodded.

"How old are you?"

Tyler pulled his shoulders back. "I just turned ten."

"Well, you're very mature for ten."

Tyler smiled.

"If you're up to it, I've got a couple of questions for you."

"I'm okay to talk."

"Are you sure?"

"Yeah."

The detective pulled out a notebook. "What time did you get home?"

"Like minutes before I called for help."

"Where were you before you came home?"

"We went to Universal Studios yesterday and came back this morning."

"Who did you go with?"

"Drew's mother took me and Jimmy."

"Their last name is?"

"Brandenberg."

Donovan jotted it down and said, "I understand from the other officer that your father is on his way."

"Yeah, he's driving from his friend's house."

"Where is that?"

"Uh, I'm not sure, but past Fort Myers, I think in Charlotte Park."

"Your mother didn't go with him?"

"No, they're divorced."

"And you live with your mother?"

"Yeah, but Dad lives, like, on the next street over. It's not so bad."

"That's good. My parents got divorced when I came out of the academy. How long have yours been divorced?"

"Around two years."

"Do you know if your mother had any enemies?"

"No. Everyone liked Mom, she's . . . was, the best."

Tyler's face crumpled. Donovan put his arm around him and pulled him in.

2

––––––––

Detective Donovan waited for Dr. Bilotti to finish his call. The medical examiner hung up and Donovan said, "I won't take too much of your time, Doc. I just want to know what the Ana Crane autopsy revealed."

"She was stabbed multiple times, I believe it was seven, to be exact, but one sliced her aorta, causing her to bleed out."

"Anything recovered from her fingernails?"

"Unfortunately, not. She had defensive wounds but didn't seem to have laid a hand on her attacker. The victim had a bruise over her right ear, which could have been done by a fist or an object not swung with excessive force. It may be that she was stunned by the blow, and it rendered her unable to resist her attacker."

"What about a time of death?"

"I'd put it somewhere between eleven p.m. and three a.m."

"Was there anything in her system?"

"We're running a toxicology panel, but no alcohol or obvious substance has been detected."

"I believe it was personal. What do you say about that?"

"Highly probable."

"There were no signs of forced entry. She either knew the killer or was duped into letting him in."

"I see you've settled on a male as the perpetrator."

"You know the stats as well as I do; three quarters of murdered females knew their killer, and a significant portion of them are current or former intimate partners."

"She was divorced, correct? Was there a significant other?"

"Yes, on both counts. I'll be talking to both her ex-husband and her boyfriend in a little while."

Donovan turned off Livingston Road and took Old Livingston Road. He glanced down Hunters Road, where Ana Crane had been stabbed to death, and made a left onto Sable Ridge Road. There was only one street separating from where the murder occurred and the block the victim's ex-husband lived on.

The homicide detective peeked between the houses as he rolled toward the one-story house Atlas Crane called home. The front yard was filled with unkempt, desert-type landscaping and a pair of scrawny tiger palms.

As Donovan approached, a neighbor's dog began yapping.

He hit the bell, and a six-foot-something strapping man opened the door.

Atlas Crane said, "Detective Donovan?"

Donovan held his badge up.

"Come in."

The detective motioned toward several cardboard boxes lining the foyer. "Did you just move in?"

"Nah, I just haven't gotten around to unpacking."

Donovan pulled out a notebook. "How long have you been here?"

"Nine months. I might just throw whatever is in them boxes out. I haven't missed them, so what's the point?"

The detective followed him into the kitchen. "True, but they could contain family memorabilia."

Crane pulled out a chair. "Yeah, well, right now ain't the time to be looking at stuff like that."

Donovan sat and set his notebook on the table. "The department sends its condolences."

"Tyler is going to miss her."

"And you?"

"It's been over for a while between us. You know, we just grew apart. You know how it is."

"How long were you married?"

"Thirteen years or so."

"It must be hard moving on after so long."

"You know what they say about men, we move on fast."

"What do you do for a living?"

"I hang drywall."

"You must be busy with all the building."

"Yeah, but you know, all these illegals we got down here take a lot of the work, and they drive prices down. It's a frigging disaster. Somebody's got to do something."

"Do you have any idea on who might have done this to Ana?"

He leaned back and pointed at Donovan. "You got to start with her new boyfriend, Fred Foster."

"What makes you say that?"

"It's a feeling I got."

"Have you met him?"

"Yeah, a lot of times, you know, when I come to get Tyler."

Donovan checked his notebook. "What don't you like about Mr. Foster?"

"He's a cocky bastard. Every time I go to the house, he's

got an attitude, thinks he's better than me or something. I mean, the guy's at *my* frigging house. Show me some damn respect. I have to wait outside like a delivery boy to see my kid?"

"Do you have joint custody?"

"I only get every other weekend, and we split up the holidays. Courts always give the mother whatever they want. Fathers don't mean shit to them."

"Besides Mr. Foster, does anyone else come to mind who would do something like this to Ana?"

"It's a crazy world; people do all kinds of sick shit. You should know that."

"I have to ask, where were you Saturday night May thirty-first through Sunday morning June first?"

"Up in Charlotte Park. I came back when Tyler called me. I was like, stunned, and drove like a maniac to get here."

"What were you doing in Charlotte Park?"

"Visiting a friend."

"What's his or her name?"

"Pete Storch. We've been friends forever. We went to grammar school together."

Donovan jotted down the alibi's contact information and left.

Driving along Airport Pulling Road, Donovan made a right onto Naples Boulevard and pulled into a space in front of the Vitamin Shoppe. He walked into the store asking for Fred Foster.

The cashier led him to the rear of the supplement seller. She knocked on a door and opened it. The area was filled with stacks of cardboard boxes. There was an earthy smell in the air.

A man in chinos and a T-shirt reading *Remember to Take*

Your Vitamins was sitting behind a metal desk. Donovan spied a pack of cigarettes on the desk, wondering about the contradiction.

The detective stepped into the unfinished space and introduced himself.

Foster jumped to his feet. "Did you get him?"

"Not yet. I need to ask you a few questions."

He collapsed into his chair. "I still can't believe it. I knew the bastard would do something crazy."

"Who are you referring to?"

"Ana's ex, Atlas Crane. He did it, he finally killed her."

"What makes you believe that?"

"How much time do you have?"

Pulling out his notebook, Donovan said, "As much as you need. Tell me what you know."

"First off, he wouldn't leave her alone. He was always coming around trying to get back with her. And he threatened Ana all the time."

"Did you hear him make a threat?"

"No. But she told me about them. At least ten different times he threatened her. Ana was afraid of him."

"Why didn't she get a restraining order against him?"

"Because of Tyler. She said she didn't want to make things weird for the kid. I didn't want to say anything, but believe me, I wish I pushed her to get one."

"Do you know if Mr. Crane ever got physical with her?"

"He sure did. It wasn't like he punched her, but she said he shoved her so hard she fell a couple of times."

"Any idea on how often this happened?"

"At least twice, if not three times, he got physical. One time he shoved her from behind, and she hit the kitchen island so hard she got a massive bruise. It was like a big purple pancake. Right here." He pointed to his side. "And another time he shoved her from her chest, and she fell backward and sprained her wrist trying to break the fall. The coward is bad news."

"When did these incidents occur?"

"The one where she hit the island wasn't that long ago. Atlas came by, saying he wanted to see Tyler, and meanwhile he knew the kid was at school and Ana was alone. After she got hurt, he said he tripped into her or some bullshit like that. After that happened she stopped letting him come in the house, even when he was legitimately there to pick up Tyler."

"Who do you consider Ana's best friends?"

Foster gave him two names and their telephone numbers.

Donovan said, "Where were you when Ana was murdered?"

"I was home. We normally spent the weekends together, but we'd had a bit of a spat, and I left around two o'clock Saturday."

"What was the fight about?"

"It wasn't a fight per se, more like a disagreement."

"I'm going to need more than that."

"Look, we were getting along great, and I thought we should move in together, but she didn't want to."

"Why was that?"

"Because of Tyler. She felt it was too soon after the divorce, but two years had gone by, and I kept telling her Tyler isn't a baby."

3

———

Donovan answered the phone on his desk. "Homicide, Detective Donovan."

"Hello, Detective. This is Pete Storch. You texted me that you were trying to get a hold of me."

The detective said, "I am. Thanks for calling me back."

"I'm sorry, but I don't answer if I don't recognize the number."

"Me neither, that's why I sent a text."

"What does the Collier County Sheriff want with me?"

"You're friends with Atlas Crane?"

"Yeah, we're sandbox friends, known each other forever. Why?"

"He said he was with you Saturday night through Sunday morning."

"He did?"

"Yes. Is that not accurate?"

"Uh, kind of."

"What does 'kind of' mean? Either he was with you or not."

"Does this have to do with what happened with his ex?"

"It may. Were you with him Saturday, May thirty-first through Sunday morning June first?"

"Atlas came up to visit, we went out, grabbed some dinner, had a couple of drinks and came back to my place."

"What time did he arrive on Saturday?"

"Late afternoon, around five."

"And when did he leave?"

"Pretty late."

"What time?"

"I think it was around midnight."

"So, Atlas arrived around five and left around midnight?"

"Yeah, that's about right."

"Okay. I appreciate your time. Have a good day."

Donovan pulled out the bottom drawer of his desk. He sat back in his chair, putting his feet on the open drawer. The detective thought over his next move since Atlas Crane's alibi had crumbled.

He reached for the ringing phone on his desk. "Homicide, Detective Donovan."

It was a uniformed officer he'd assigned to knock on doors. He said, "Looks like we got a witness in the Crane murder."

Donovan swung his feet to the ground. "What do you have?"

"A neighbor across the street. He said he saw the ex-husband, Atlas Crane, using the keypad for the garage to get into the house in the middle of the night."

"Perfect. Bring him in."

"Hold on, there' s more."

Donovan stood. "Go ahead."

"This guy, Owen Reale, he was out walking his dog, said the dog had the runs or something, and he had to take him out again about an hour later, and he saw the ex-husband coming out of the garage. And get this, he thinks he was carrying a knife."

"What time was this?"

"He said the first time he went out it was two fifteen, and the second time about an hour later."

"Is he certain it was Atlas Crane?"

"Yes, he said no doubt about it. He said he's lived there for ten years and knew him well."

"Did he say anything else about Crane?"

"He said he used to socialize with him a little, but he backed off, said Crane has a temper."

"Get him to come in as soon as possible. We need to get his statement on record."

"You think the husband did it, right?"

"Let's see how Crane responds to this."

Donovan looked at the video feed from the interview room. Legs splayed, Atlas Crane was sitting with his hand over his crotch. Sworn statement and laptop in hand, the detective swung the door open and took a seat opposite Crane.

"Hey, how long is this going to take? I got to pick up Tyler."

"That depends on you, Mr. Crane."

"What are you talking about?"

"You claimed to be with your friend Peter Storch in Charlotte Park the night your ex-wife was murdered."

"I was."

"Not according to your friend. He said you left before midnight."

"That's right, I did leave around then."

"Well, that left plenty of time to get to your ex's house at the time of her death."

"I didn't do anything to her. I wasn't there."

"Where were you between midnight and the time your son called you?"

"I left Pete's house, and it was late, and we'd had a few pops. I was tired and pulled over into a rest stop and slept. I didn't wake up till Tyler called me. I guess I was more tired than I thought."

"You're telling me you fell asleep in a rest area for what? Ten hours?"

"Like I said, I was dead tired."

"What rest stop?"

"Uh, the first one on Route 75 after I got on."

"Are you sure about that?"

"Yeah, pretty sure it was the first one."

"Did you interact with anyone there?"

"No. I was sleeping."

Donovan opened the folder in front of him and slid a document toward Atlas Crane. "We have a sworn statement by someone who saw you use the garage to gain entry into your wife's house at the time she died."

"That's bullshit."

Donovan opened his laptop and tapped on its keyboard. He turned the screen around and hit enter. "We have a Ring Doorbell video from the house across the street from your wife's. That's you entering the code to the garage door."

Atlas leaned forward. "No way. You can't see shit."

Donovan arched his arm and opened a second video. "This is you leaving. It's 2:15 a.m. The medical examiner put the time of death between 1 and 2 a.m., Sunday morning, June first."

"Come on, man. How can you say that's me? You can't see shit."

Donovan slapped the laptop shut. "Admit it, Mr. Crane, you killed your ex-wife."

"I didn't do anything to her."

"Look, this is your one shot at leniency. If you confess, you'll save the taxpayers money on a trial, and the prosecutors will go easier on you."

"I ain't confessing to nothing. I want a lawyer."

Donovan took a chair in front of prosecutor O'Leary's desk. "I want an arrest warrant for Atlas Crane for the murder of his ex-wife, Ana."

"Lay out the motivation for homicide."

"As you know, they were recently divorced, and it was her decision to split up. She took on a boyfriend, and by all accounts it was getting serious. There was talk of them moving in together. This upset Atlas Crane, which we believe was the motivation for taking her life."

"Do you believe it was premeditated?"

"He went to her house in the middle of the night. There's the slimmest of chances he went there to try to win her back, but why use the garage? And he denies being there, so that kills the reconciliation angle."

"That might qualify as premeditation."

"We have a friend of the deceased who told us that Ana and Atlas Crane had a bad argument the day before."

"Okay. What do we have on the husband as the perpetrator?"

"We have a witness, a neighbor who was walking his dog saw him enter and leave through the garage. He said it was Crane and that he was holding what he believed was a knife. We also have a doorbell video of someone by the garage. The time fits, but it's difficult to make an ID for certain, but the build of the man matches Crane. Oh, and Crane fabricated an alibi."

"The witness is going to testify?"

"Definitely. He knows Crane well and isn't a fan, said he has anger issues."

"It'd be nice to flesh that out further, maybe there are others who can testify to his anger."

"We're working on developing more evidence."

"Are there any other suspects?"

"No. We ruled out anyone else, including her current boyfriend, who Crane said we should look at."

"All right, keep working on obtaining additional evidence."

"We're on it. I feel good about getting more."

"Okay, we'll move forward with the arrest warrant."

PART II

ONE YEAR AFTER ANA CRANE'S MURDER

Trial – noun: a formal examination of evidence by a judge, typically before a jury, in order to decide guilt in a case of criminal or civil proceedings.

4

———————

DETECTIVE DONOVAN APPROACHED THE COURTHOUSE. IT WAS day two of Atlas Crane's murder trial. Both sides had presented opening statements the previous morning, and the state had begun laying out its case later that afternoon.

Donovan had felt good about his testimony and of the others who'd been on the stand yesterday.

Today, the dog-walking neighbor, who'd seen Atlas Crane enter and leave through the garage, would testify. Several others would also bear witness, including the murdered woman's boyfriend, as to the fighting between the couple.

The dozen reporters hanging outside the entrance spied Donovan and began to converge around him, shouting questions.

"Come on, guys, you know I'm not going to comment."

Donovan pushed through the door and stood in the line forming for the body scanner. He pulled his ringing phone out. It was the office.

The detective said, "Hey, what's going on?"

"Bad news, boss."

Donovan stiffened. "What happened?"

"Owen Reale was killed in a car crash this morning."

A key witness was dead. Donovan stepped out of the line. "Are you shitting me?"

"No. It happened around 8 a.m. on Livingston Road. Everybody drives way too fast on that—"

Donovan cupped his hand over the phone. "We're screwed."

"That's what I thought."

"I've got to talk to O'Leary."

Donovan took his badge out and cut to the front of the line. "Excuse me. I'm on official business."

Prosecutor O'Leary was seated at the right-hand counsel table. Donovan entered the courtroom's well and tapped O'Leary on the shoulder.

"We have a big problem."

"What happened?"

Donovan lowered his voice. "Owen Reale died in a car crash this morning."

O'Leary swiveled his head, surveying the area. "Christ! That blows a giant hole in our case."

"Is there any way we can get his sworn statement entered into evidence?"

"No."

"Are you sure? This guy just died this morning."

"Defendants have the right to challenge their accusers. There's no way any judge would allow it in."

"What can we do?"

"Nothing. We'll press on and hope what we have is enough."

"Do you think it's going to be enough to convict?"

"It always depends on the jury. You never know what they're thinking with any certainty."

"What is your gut telling you?"

"Without the eyewitness putting Crane at the house at the time of death, I'd say it's fifty-fifty, at best."

5

Two days later, Atlas Crane burst through the doors of the courthouse into the sunshine. Microphones in hand, a dozen reporters rushed toward him, asking for comments on the verdict.

He leaned toward a mic with the WINK news logo on it. "Today the jury agreed with what I was saying all along. I had nothing to do with what happened to Ana, and the verdict proves I was unfairly targeted by the police. Ana's killer is still out there. I'm hoping the sheriff finally gets the message and gets his, uh, backside moving to find who did this."

"What are you going to do next?"

Atlas swung his arm around his son Tyler's shoulders. "I'm going to be the best father I can be. This sham of a trial put a ton of strain on my son and me. Now it's time for us to get on with our lives."

"You've been quoted, at least twice, saying that you were intending to sue the county. Is that something you're going to follow through on?"

"We just want Ana's killer brought to justice. If they do that, then we'll move on."

"Tyler! How do you feel about the verdict?"

"I knew Daddy didn't do anything wrong, and I'm so happy this is over."

"Come on, son, let's get out of here."

As Atlas and Tyler headed to the parking lot, prosecutor O'Leary came out of the courthouse. The gaggle of reporters converged on him.

"Are you surprised by the verdict?"

"We're disappointed. We felt we put on a strong enough case, but the jury didn't agree."

"Is there anything you'd do differently?"

"Well, we were hobbled by the untimely death of a crucial witness, an eyewitness who could have put Mr. Crane at the scene. If he'd been able to testify, we believe the jury would have come to a different conclusion."

PART III

PRESENT DAY

Revenge – noun: an act or instance of retaliation in order to get even.

6

———

I SPED DOWN ROUTE 41, SLOWING TO MAKE THE TURN INTO Pelican Marsh. Ray Larson wanted to see me, and I was trying to squeeze it in before a day at the beach with Laura.

The guard waved me through, and I navigated to an enclave of single-family homes named The Arbors. I pulled down a sun visor to block the reflection off a lake and made a left onto Larson's street.

Larson was not only a friend and lawyer, but he was also responsible for most of the jobs I'd taken on. His discreet web of contacts provided cases where justice had failed miserably. Plus, he had dependable connections to use when I needed help.

His house was understated, like he was. Larson had earned an eight-figure fee from a medical malpractice case he'd won for a client but lived well below his means and took pleasure in the simpler things in life. It was difficult to understand how he'd adjusted to life after his wife had died of cancer. How he avoided the bitterness of loss was something to try and learn from.

Larson opened the door with a smile. "Hello, Beck, come on in."

"How's it going, Ray?"

"Wonderful, another great day in paradise."

I followed him into the kitchen. "How come you're not at the beach?"

"I've got a noon tee off at La Playa. I'm playing with John Morgan."

The personal injury lawyer was all over the TV. "Ugh. I can't stand his commercials."

"Me neither, but he's been useful. He referred the last two cases you handled."

"Really?"

"Yes. You want anything to drink?"

"No thanks. What did you want to see me about?"

Larson picked a thick folder off the island's white countertop. "A friend of a friend asked me to speak with a Tyler Crane."

Larson was as smooth as silk, but something was off. "What friend of a friend?"

"A female friend."

"You went on a date?"

"Yes, but it was social, not romantic."

I chuckled. "It's okay, Ray. I'm just busting."

"I'm serious, since Kay died, I really have no interest."

"You can't be a monk."

"I'm not. I'm always out. It's just that as far as women are concerned, no one can replace Kay."

"You don't have to replace her, it's about, you know, having companionship."

Larson snorted. "Look who's giving relationship advice. You don't let anybody in."

"Me and Laura are doing good. We're going to Clam Pass today."

"Great. I like her, you should find a way to make this work. You're good for each other."

I pointed to the folder. "What's the file about?"

"Like I said, Tyler Crane came to me through a friend, and it's a sad story. His mother was murdered fourteen years ago, and the police pinned it on his father, Atlas Crane."

My shoulders tensed. My mother had been killed as well, but at the hands of a career criminal, not my father. "And?"

He handed the file to me. "You'll have to read the transcript of the trial, but the father wasn't convicted."

"And fourteen years later, the son wants to get even?"

He nodded. "Read the file and meet with Tyler. He's a nice young man and has the funding from an inheritance. I believe you'll find it interesting."

I rented a setup at the beach and settled onto a chaise lounge. A soft breeze was blowing, and, under the shade of an umbrella, it couldn't get any better.

Laura reached over and took my hand. "See how nice this is?"

"It's a good thing we got an umbrella."

"You want to take a dip?"

"Maybe later."

"Do you want to take a walk?"

"Not now."

"Where do you want to eat later?"

She was a machine gun loaded with questions. "Wherever you want."

"Maybe we'll go to True Food. What do you think?"

"If you want, but if you want something good, I'll grill something at the house."

"Sounds good. You want to stop at Whole Foods on the way back?"

What I wanted was for her to stop asking questions.

"Sure."

I opened the file Larson had given me.

"What are you doing?"

"I have to read something for work."

She bolted upright. "I'm going for a walk."

I wanted to tell her to grow up, but the last time I did that, it took months to close the wound. Laura was great. Was it me? I'd fended for myself since being shoved into foster care. The only one I was close with was my foster brother, Mario, and 80 percent of the time I had to look out for him.

A car length away, a young couple was digging in the sand with their toddler. I shook away the idea it could be me one day and started reading.

I took Pine Ridge Road west, where it turned into Seagate Drive. Snaking around on Seagate, I pulled over just before public access was denied.

Walking a couple of yards along the edge of Venetian Bay, I spied Tyler Crane sitting on a bench overlooking the water.

He started when I came up behind him, saying, "Tyler?"

"You scared me." He stood. "Mr. Beck?"

"Yep. Just Beck though. Sit down."

"I didn't know this place existed. It's quiet down here."

"But it gets busy during season."

"What doesn't?"

"You're right. Tell me what's on your mind."

"Well, I told Mr. Larson all about it."

"I'd like to hear it from you directly."

"Everything?"

"Yes."

Tyler explained how he'd found his mother dead. He and I shared an experience I wouldn't wish on anyone. I never jumped into any case, but I knew it'd be hard not to help him.

"I'm sorry about your mother."

"Thanks. I'm not going to lie, it was rough, and then the cops arrested my father."

"I read the transcript of the trial. But what did you think about it?"

"At the time, there was no way I could believe my father had killed Mom. I was just ten years old, and, you know, my whole life was turned upside down."

I knew the feeling. "You were living with your mother when it happened. Did you go to live with your father afterward?"

"Yeah, I mean, our house was a crime scene, and who would want to stay there anyway? And my father lived really close by. My Aunt Pamela, she's my mom's sister, wanted me to stay with her, but my dad said no."

"Who did you think killed your mother?"

"At the time, I didn't know. It was scary, I thought it was random or something."

"And now?"

He frowned. "My father did it."

"What changed your mind?"

"I didn't want to believe it, plus I was just a kid. I mean, you trust your father, right?"

"Of course. But when and why the change?"

"Well, I started to realize the real man my father was as I got older. He was mean and had a bad temper. He'd lose it over the littlest things."

"That doesn't make him a murderer."

"Before I get into it, now I can see I ignored a lot of signs. I mean, it's only natural, right? I was just too young to put it together."

"Of course. What kind of things?"

"Well, they fought a lot, and he'd get physical, you know? And like two years after my mom died, my father started going out with this woman, Katy. She was nice and all, but they'd fight a lot too, and one time, I was in the garage working on my bike, and they were going at it, and he said something to her like, '*You better watch your effing self, or you'll end up like my ex.*'"

"What else made you change your mind?"

"I always asked him why the police thought it was him, and he said they had nothing on him. That it was what the cops did because most of the time when a woman was killed it was her husband or boyfriend who did it. I checked on the internet, and it was true, so I never questioned it. I guess it was what I wanted to believe. And then at the trial they really didn't have anything more. The doorbell video wasn't good, you couldn't tell who it was."

"It sounds like there's more to come."

"Well, I got a call from a reporter for the *Daily News* because it was coming up on the fourteen-year anniversary of the murder, and what he told me made me realize my father did it."

"What did he tell you?"

7

———

Tyler looked me in the eye. "I never knew there was an eyewitness who died before he could testify. He was in a crash and was killed, I think, the day he was going to get on the stand. I was like, blown away and called the prosecutor who handled the case."

"You spoke to O'Leary?"

"Yes. And he said the witness had been a neighbor. I remembered him. He lived across the street from my mom's house. His dog was sick that night, and he was out walking it a lot. He saw my father open the garage door in the middle of the night, and then he saw him leave right after my mom was murdered. Plus, he said my father was holding a knife."

"That would have been powerful testimony."

"I can't believe the judge wouldn't allow the jury to know what our neighbor saw. The prosecutor said you have to be able to confront someone who accuses you. I get it, but this was crazy, it's so unfair."

"It would have put your father there at the time of death, but the defense would have tried to discredit him. How old was this man?"

"I think he'd be about eighty now."

"So, he would have been around his mid-sixties. Did he wear glasses?"

"Yes."

"And this was at night, and I'm sure he saw him from a distance. The defense would have been all over this."

"But there was this doorbell video from that night. It's not the greatest, but it confirms the time the neighbor said he saw my father there."

Tyler held his phone out and played a grainy video. I took it and zoomed in. "You can't make out who it is."

"I know, but I can tell it's my father. And look at the time. It's got to be him."

An idea hit me. "I'm going to email a copy of this to myself."

"Sure. What are you thinking?"

"At this point, nothing. I need to do some research first. Tell me something about your father."

"Like what?"

"His interests, hobbies. What does he enjoy doing?"

"Oh, that's easy, it's being on the water. He loves to fish and just cruise around."

"He has a boat?"

"Yeah, not a big one. I think it's an eighteen-footer. He bought it used. I've only been out twice on that one."

"He's really into it?"

"Yeah, he even made me go out with him on the boat we had at the time, like two days after Mom was killed. I didn't want to go, but he said he had to clear his mind. I think he went out to get rid of the knife he used to kill her with."

"What makes you say that?"

"He was acting strange that day, and I saw him slip his hand in the water. It looked like he was dropping something in the water."

"Where was this?"

"That's the thing. You know, my whole life, my father always said you had to respect the water and that no boat is bigger than the ocean. I would always want to go into the Gulf, but unless the water was glass, we never did. But that day, right after my mom died, the water wasn't calm at all, but he went out all the way into Gordon's Pass, and that's when I saw him drop something in the water. It had to be the knife."

"Did you see the knife?"

"No. But I really think that's what it was. I've thought a lot about this over the years, and I'm ninety-nine percent sure about it."

The back-and-forth currents at the pass leading to the Gulf would carry and bury anything dropped into it. Searching for a murder weapon would be futile.

"Would you say your father was smart?"

"He didn't go to college, but he's definitely street-smart."

My brother from another mother, Mario, was sitting at one of Taberna Burntwood's outdoor tables.

I approached, pulling out a chair. "How's it going?"

"Can't complain. Let's get a drink."

His eyes were glassy. I said, "Did you got a head start on me?"

"No. I didn't have anything."

"Lay off the weed, bro."

"Don't worry about me."

"You know what they said in rehab."

"Okay, Daddy."

"Come on, Mario. I'm only looking out for you. We have to watch out for each other."

"I don't have a problem anymore. I dealt with it, so leave me alone, okay?"

I nodded, hoping he wasn't kidding himself.

Mario raised his hand to flag a waiter and said, "What happened with the kid you met?"

A server came right over. Mario ordered a beer, and though I would've liked a Tito's vodka on the rocks, I asked for a seltzer.

"The kid's case has a little similarity to what happened to us."

"Like what?"

"His mother was murdered, and it looks like it was the father. Given that my mom was killed by a lifetime criminal out on bail, I feel for the kid."

"And my mother was a crackhead."

It may have been where Mario picked up his tendency to overdo things. "I guess I was trying to say he lost his mother at an early age, like we did. Anyway, his father went on trial for the killing and got off, but if you can believe it, an eyewitness died on the morning he was supposed to testify."

Our drinks were delivered. Mario took a long pull on his brew before asking, "Was it suspicious?"

"That was my first reaction, but it was a car accident. And the other driver was an older lady who'd just lost her husband and was obviously distracted."

"Crazy. If the eyewitness would've testified, would the father have been convicted?"

"That's the trillion-dollar question. The witness saw him entering the house through the garage and leaving the same way at the time of death. The witness also claimed the kid's old man was holding a knife when he saw him leave."

"Was this witness reliable?"

"He seemed to be."

"What do you want to do?"

"The kid gave me a doorbell video, but it's inconclusive."

"Why don't we see what Larson's son can do with it? He's a tech magician."

"I already sent it to him. Why don't you chat up the homicide guys at the sheriff's office?"

"Donovan owes me a little bit. I fed him info on that motel stabbing."

"Good. Tommy said he'd jump on the doorbell video right away. Do you think you can get something out of Donovan today?"

"Sure thing. I'll talk to him and stop by your place tonight."

"Uh, Laura's coming over."

"So?"

"She's on my back about working too much, not enough alone time, blah, blah, blah."

"Why doesn't she just move in with you?"

I shrugged. "I don't know if I'm ready for that."

"Just do it, man. What's the worst thing that could happen? If it doesn't work, you bounce out of it."

"I'm not like you. I don't want to go through all that if it isn't going to last."

"Nobody has a crystal ball, man. Give it a shot. It don't work out, you move on."

"I just can't live with somebody and—"

"What are you talking about? That's what we did in foster care. How many times did we move?"

He was right, and maybe that was the reason I was reluctant. "Too many." I stood. "I've got to hop, we'll talk later."

8

As she put a dish in the sink, Laura said, "That pork chop was really good."

"I'm glad you liked it."

"It's nice that you want to cook for me instead of going out all the time."

"I like going out to dinner, but it's nice staying home too."

"Let me take care of the dishes."

I shook my head. "I got it. See if there is anything to watch on Netflix."

"I doubt it. Most of the new stuff is foreign, and the acting and dubbing is terrible."

"Some of the French and Italian ones are pretty good. They have highly developed cinema industries."

She turned on the TV. "I know, but I don't like reading captions."

"Me neither, but if it's a good story, you get used to it."

"Oh, look, there's a *House Hunters* in Naples on."

"What price range?"

"It's for coach homes, around five hundred thousand."

"You should watch it, get an idea of the market. Your lease renewal is coming up, and it makes sense to buy something."

Her face darkened.

"What's the matter?"

"Nothing."

Why did people say that when something was bothering them? "Tell me what's wrong. All I was trying to do was—"

"Forget it. I thought, you know, things were going good with us."

I shut the faucet. "They are. So?"

"I thought maybe we might, you know, move in together."

"Oh. But your lease is up in like two months."

"It is."

"That's right around the corner."

"Forget it, okay."

"Come on. That's not fair. You bring it up out of thin air, and I'm the bad guy?"

"Thin air? So, you never even thought about it?"

"A little bit. I just need more time."

"If this isn't going anywhere, tell me now so I have a chance to have a family."

"I don't understand how all this came up. We were having a great time, and now you're giving me an ultimatum?"

"Look, we're both facing the biological clock. I don't want to have trouble conceiving, and I don't want to be in my mid-forties with an infant."

She went from moving in together to having a baby. "Can we take this one step at a time?"

"We've been together for almost two years. I'm not a kid."

"I get it, but things are better now, right?"

She shrugged.

I said, "Come on, you know they are. I know it's my fault,

but, you know, after what I went through, it takes me a while to get comfortable."

"It's been two years. We're not teenagers. I need to know where this is going."

"Just give me a couple of months."

"My lease is coming due, I can't just—"

"Renew it and then we'll break it. I'll pay the penalty, no problem if things don't work out."

Her cell phone rang. "It's my mom. My aunt's in the hospital."

"I hope she's all right." The irony of being saved by a potential mother-in-law was not lost on me.

Laura plopped onto the couch as she talked to her mother, and I retreated to the lanai. I put my phone on the table and watched a family of ducks paddle on the lake.

Why were relationships so hard? Things were going good with Laura, but could I take the next step?

My cell rattled and I answered it. "Hey, Mario. How did you make out with Detective Donovan?"

"He wasn't receptive at first, so, I had to work my magic."

"What did he say?"

"Donovan said he believes Atlas Crane stabbed his ex-wife to death."

"What kind of evidence did they have?"

"The two of them had been arguing, and Crane lied about his alibi. Atlas said he was up in Charlotte Park with a friend, but he left earlier than he said with enough time to get there at the time of death. Donovan said he confronted him over it, and Atlas gave him some bullshit that he pulled into a rest area and fell asleep."

"What about the witness who died in the car crash?"

"Donovan said the guy's story checked out, and he believes

if the guy had been able to testify that Atlas would have been convicted."

"Really?"

"Yep, that's what he said. Oh yeah, he also said they found a drop of blood on the driveway. It was right by the garage, and it matched the dead woman's blood."

"Probably dripped off the knife the neighbor said Crane was carrying."

"Definitely."

I said, "This guy really got away with it."

"So, we're taking this job, right?"

I pawed my chin. "I'm not sure yet."

"We haven't had anything for ages. Come on, let's do it."

"I'm not ready to commit yet."

"Come on, this is a good one."

"We have to be sure."

"We are. Even the cops said he did it."

"Right now, what I'm thinking of, to get back at this guy would be the baddest-assed thing we've ever done. I want to be sure there's no doubt it was the father."

"How are you going to get better info than Donovan and the trial transcript?"

"I've got an idea. Let me make a call and I'll get back to you."

9

I PLOPPED ON THE COUCH AFTER LAURA LEFT TO VISIT HER aunt in the hospital. Reaching for the remote, my phone rang. It was Larson's kid returning my call.

"Hey, Tommy, how are things in the special effects world?"

"Busy as hell. I tell ya, I could double the size of the business if I wanted to."

"You should do it."

"Nah, I enjoy the creative side too much. If this place gets any bigger, I'd be nothing but a manager, pushing paper instead of designing things."

"I get it. What are you working on now?"

"MGM, actually they're Amazon these days, is doing a movie where a massive earthquake cracks open the permafrost. Scientists discover a whole slew of prehistoric animals in the ice, like saber-tooth tigers, and can make them come to life."

It sounded like a twist on *Jurassic Park* and something I'd never watch. "That sounds interesting and scary."

"It's been done before, but that's Hollywood for you; they get a winning formula and beat it to death."

"That's so true. But at least it's work for you."

"It's not particularly challenging, but we got to make about fifty creatures and the special vehicles the scientists use to uncover and move them."

"Since you mentioned vehicles, I've got to say, we're still talking about the car thing you did for us. It was amazing."

"Thanks. I'm glad it worked out for you and my dad."

"You're a lifesaver. What did you think about the video I sent you? Can you do something with it?"

"For sure. I ran it through a new AI-powered tool we just bought."

"Expensive?"

"Yeah, but cutting-edge tech always is. I gotta say it's worth it. AI did a great job cleaning and enhancing it. I also brightened it with another piece of software we have."

Toby began circling the kitchen. He needed to go out to do his business. "Thanks, man."

"I'm going to toy around with it some more before sending it back to you."

"How does it look?"

"Pretty good, but I can make it better."

"Can you do me a favor and send it now?"

"Sure. Just give me around twenty minutes. I've got to finish something before it dries."

After the call ended, I grabbed Toby's leash.

"Come on, boy."

Toby tugged me down the driveway, raising a leg on the light pole at the curb. When he was done, he headed toward the preserve. I opened the gate and took his leash off. He trotted a car length and squatted. Taking a poop bag out as he relieved himself, I noticed his ears stand up.

Picking up what he'd left, I watched Toby bound into the woods.

"Toby!"

I hustled after him. "Come here, boy!"

He started barking. It was coming from the left. I followed him to a small clearing. Toby was yelping at a cardboard box the size of a refrigerator. Its top was draped with a blue tarp.

"Easy, boy."

He stopped barking and I heard a baby cry.

I snapped the leash back on Toby's collar and approached the box. "Hello? Is anyone in there?"

A female voice said, "Please leave us alone."

I lifted the cardboard flap. A girl, around sixteen, and a baby were huddled inside. A duffel bag, backpack, and a gallon water jug lined one side of the box.

"Go away, please!"

I did a double take. She looked like Bev, my foster sister. "I'm not here to hurt you. My name is Beck, and this guy is Toby. He's harmless."

She pulled the baby to her chest but said nothing.

"Are you okay? Can I help you with anything?"

"Just leave us alone."

"You don't have to be afraid. I'm just trying to help you."

"I know."

"What's your name?"

"Dawn."

"And is that your baby?"

"Yes. She's Abby."

"She's beautiful."

Dawn weakly said, "She sure is."

"Are you staying in here?"

She nodded.

"What happened?"

"I got kicked out of my foster home when I had Abby."

"How long have you been here?"

"This is our second night."

"Are you hungry?"

She shrugged.

Pointing in the direction of my house, I said, "I live right over there. I've got plenty of food."

"We're okay."

"You can't stay here. It's dangerous. There are bears and snakes and even bobcats roaming through here. You and Abby aren't safe."

"We'll be okay."

"It's supposed to downpour later and rain the next couple of days. This cardboard isn't going to hold up. Your baby is going to get sick."

She tucked the blanket under her baby's neck and reached under the mat she was sitting on. "I have more plastic."

"Where are you going to get something to eat? Doesn't she need special formula and diapers?"

Her lip began quivering.

I knelt. "Look, come with me. I have a refrigerator full of food. You can wash up and eat."

She wiped a tear off her cheek. "Why are you being so nice to us?"

"Because I know what it's like to be homeless. I was in foster care for years, and I know it sounds crazy, but me and Mario ran away when we were sixteen. That's how I ended up in Florida."

Her eyes widened. "You were in foster care?"

"Yes. In New Jersey. My mother was murdered, and my father drank himself to death. I was in four different homes." I turned my head, fingering the scar behind my ear. "Trust me, I know how bad it can be in some of those places."

"What happened?"

"Come on, I'll tell you about it, and about Mario. He was the only good thing to come out of being in a foster home."

She hesitated before rising. "Who is Mario?"

"My brother from another mother."

She frowned. "I met a friend in a group home, but we were split up and I never saw her again."

I grabbed her duffel bag and backpack. "You can use my washing machine."

"Thanks."

"No problem. You know, you look like a foster sister I had in Jersey."

"Really?"

"Yeah, the resemblance is crazy."

10

———

APPROACHING MY HOUSE, I SAID, "I KNOW THIS HAS TO FEEL weird for you, so, if you'd rather hang out on the lanai, I'll grab some food and bring it out to you."

Dawn studied my face before whispering, "If I can, I'd really like to give Abby a bath and maybe wash some clothes, if it's okay."

"That's fine. You can use the bathroom next to the kitchen." I raised her bags. "I'll throw a wash on and make something to eat."

She hung her head. "Thank you, you're so nice, thank you."

I opened the door and stepped inside. "Come on in." I pointed. "The bathroom is to the right."

"This is a nice house."

"Thanks. Uh, does Abby have a bottle or a cup that needs to be washed?"

She dug a heavily used baby bottle out of a pocket.

Taking it from her, I said, "I don't know anything about shots and stuff babies need, but when was the last time she saw a doctor?"

"I took her to a clinic a couple of weeks ago."

"A good friend of mine is a doctor. I can see if I can get him to come by today or tomorrow just to be sure she's all right."

"No. I can take her to the clinic."

"It won't cost anything. He owes me a couple of favors."

She shrugged.

"Go wash up and think about it."

"Thank you so much."

"No problem. You know, I gotta say it again, you really look like someone I used to know."

"I do?"

My cell rang. "Yes, it's crazy. I have to get this, it's my girlfriend."

I opened the slider and went onto the lanai. "Hey, Laura. You're not going to believe this, I was walking Toby, and he went into the preserve at the end of the block and found a girl and her baby living in a refrigerator box."

"What? By your house?"

"Yeah, in the preserve. I was, like, stunned. Toby started barking at the box, and I went over, and there they were. It's crazy, the baby is really young."

"What were they doing there?"

"Just huddled up. The girl said she was kicked out of the foster home they were in. She said after she gave birth, the foster father mistreated her and threw her out."

"That's terrible."

"And it happens way too often. I'm getting them something to eat, and I'm going to see if I can get Dr. Elias to check out the baby."

"Oh, that's good."

"You think you could pick up some diapers? I'll pay for them."

"Sure. What size diapers?"

"Diapers have sizes?"

"Of course they do. Is she a newborn?"

"I think so. Maybe a couple of months old."

"Okay. What about clothes? Do they need some?"

"Good thinking. That would be great. The mother is about your size."

"I'll pick up a couple of things at Walmart."

"Great. Thanks."

"I'll bring them right over."

"Cool."

I threw some chopped meat in the microwave and turned the grill on. After it thawed out, I seasoned it and made hamburgers. I put them on the barbecue and went back inside. As I was sautéing green beans and onions, Dawn came out of the bathroom. She was carrying Abby. The baby was wrapped in a towel and fast asleep.

Dawn said, "It smells good."

"I have a couple of burgers on the grill for you. What do you feed Abby?"

"Baby food."

"Do you have any?"

She cast her eyes down and shook her head.

"Don't worry. Laura, my girlfriend, she's getting you some diapers. I'll tell her to pick up some baby food. Anything in particular?"

She looked at her baby. "Abby loves applesauce, if, if she can get it."

"No problem." I called Laura and asked her to get the baby food.

"Laura's in Walmart, she'll be here in a few minutes."

She blinked away a tear. "I don't know what to say."

"There's nothing to say, just relax. Why don't you sit on the lanai?"

She eyed the couch, and I said, "Or you can watch TV if you want."

She took a step toward the family room, and I picked up the remote and clicked the TV on. "Here you go, put whatever you like on."

I opened the slider as a crack of thunder sounded. "Looks like you made the right choice." I pointed to a flash of lightning. "It's going to rain."

Dawn frowned.

"Don't worry. You can stay here. I have four bedrooms. You can take one and stay as long as you need."

"I can't."

"Why not? Stay, and tomorrow we can see about getting you some assistance from the county. I can help you with that."

She sniffled.

"It's okay. I know what it's like. Just take it easy, you'll see. You and little Abby will be safe. I promise."

Dawn kissed Abby's head and the baby cooed.

"See? She's happy you landed here. Wait until Laura brings the baby food, she'll be even better."

"You're too nice."

"Don't worry about it, I know what it's like to be on your own. You'll stay here until we get you some assistance."

"But—"

"No buts. Come here, let me show you your room, and then you can eat."

I swung open the door to a spare bedroom. "You can use this one. It has its own bathroom."

She softly said, "It's the nicest room I ever had."

"I hope you and Abby will be comfortable. Oh, we have to get her a crib for her to sleep in."

"It's okay. There's tons of room in the bed."

"It might be safer, you know, you could roll on her when you're sleeping."

"It's not a big deal."

"How about one of those bassinet things?"

She shrugged.

"Come on, we'll look them up online and see what's out there." I laughed. "I don't know much about taking care of babies."

She held Abby out. "Here, hold her."

"Uh, I don't know."

"I have to go to the bathroom."

"Okay." I stiffened. "Give her to me."

"If she knows you're scared, she'll cry."

I dropped my shoulders and took Abby from her. "She's so light."

"I gotta go."

She headed to the bathroom, and rocking Abby, I whispered, "Everything is going to be all right, little one."

The doorbell rang. I shifted Abby onto the left side of my chest and opened the door.

Arms full of bags, Laura's eyes widened. "Oh my God. The baby's here? Where's the mother?"

"She's in the bathroom."

"You let them in the house?"

"I couldn't let them stay outside, it's going to pour later."

"They moved in?"

"Just until she gets on her feet."

"Are you kidding me?"

"No. What's the big deal, they're harmless."

"How can you say that? You don't know them."

"It's a girl with a baby." I chuckled. "I think I can handle whatever they throw at me."

Laura scoffed, brushing past me to set a package of diapers on the counter.

"How much do I owe you?"

"A hundred and thirty."

I set the baby on the couch and took a wad of cash out of my pocket. I peeled off a hundred and a fifty. "Thanks, I really appreciate you picking this stuff up."

"I wouldn't of went if I knew she'd be moving in with you."

"What? I don't understand."

Laura hissed, "You freak out when I mention moving in together? And then you take them in?"

Was it jealousy or a genuine safety concern? "I, I just was trying to help them. You can't have a baby living in the woods."

At the sound of the toilet flushing, Laura leaned closer, saying, "So, you find some girl in the preserve, and you invite her in your house? What are you going to do, round up every homeless person and have them live with you? You're letting people take advantage of you."

I wanted to recite the stoic saying that kindness was a strength, not a weakness.

"Come on, Laura! You don't—"

Dawn walked into the kitchen, saying, "I'm sorry. We're going to leave. You've been nice enough, I don't want to cause any trouble."

Her arms out for Abby, I handed off her baby. "It's okay. Laura, this is Dawn. Dawn, this is Laura."

Dawn eked out a hello.

Laura smiled. "Nice to meet you. Your baby is precious."

I looked at Laura in amazement. Mr. Hyde had morphed into Dr. Jekyll. I said, "She really is, and she doesn't cry, she's so quiet."

Laura said, "I picked up some baby food and diapers."

Abby cried.

Dawn said, "Thanks so much. Abby's hungry. If it's okay, I'll feed her, then we'll leave."

I said, "Stay. It's raining, and you have to eat too."

"I don't want to cause any—"

"You're staying until we get you assistance from the county."

She looked at Laura, who said, "It's fine."

"Are you sure? I don't want to get in the way."

"Yes, it's really no problem. I have to get going anyway."

11

———————

A BLUE FEELING CAME OVER ME AS DAWN WOLFED DOWN THREE burgers. I knew what it was like to eat more than you normally would. A stockpiling mentality took over when you had no idea when the next meal was coming.

Clearing the table, I said, "I've got to make a couple of calls. Why don't you watch some TV?"

"I'm really beat. I haven't been sleeping much."

That wasn't surprising. "No problem. Go lie down."

She took Abby to the spare bedroom, and I retreated to the den. It took four rings for Laura to pick up. But she didn't say anything.

I said, "Hey, how are you doing?"

"Fine."

"How come you didn't hang out?"

"I didn't feel like it."

"Don't tell me you're mad because I'm helping Dawn and her baby."

"I went out and got baby food and diapers for them."

"I know, thanks. What's wrong, then?"

She hesitated. "You never told me she was moving in with you."

"She's not moving in. What was I supposed to do? Let them live in a box? In the rain?"

"You should've told me she was in your house. You made it seem like she was in the woods."

"If they were in the box, I'd be all right with you?"

She went quiet.

"Come on, Laura. I'm just trying to help them. You don't know what it's like to be totally on your own. I do."

"You always throw that in my face."

"What are you talking about? I never say that."

"You got all evasive when I mentioned moving in together, and then you just spin around and invite them to move in."

"It's a completely different thing."

"No, it's not."

"You're dead wrong, but I'm not going to argue with you."

"I've got to go."

"Wait a—"

The line went dead. I was about to hit redial when an email from Tommy, Larson's son, chimed in. I opened it and clicked on the MP4 attachment.

Full-screening the video, I hit play. I watched it three times, slowing and freezing frames several times.

I checked the time and sent a text to Mario before making a call.

Larson picked up on the first ring. "Hello, Beck. It's late, is everything all right?"

"Yes. I just have a couple of things to tell you. Is it a good time or too late?"

"It's fine, I just finished a book."

"What did you read?"

"*The Frontiersmen.* It's a true account of the men who

settled in mid-America, a beautiful but deadly area at the time. They battled Indians and built cities. It's one of the best books I've read in a long time."

"I'll have to check it out."

"I'll give it to you."

That meant I had to read it. "Thanks."

"So, what's on your mind?"

"To start"—I lowered my voice—"I need some help with a county contact who can fast-track social services paperwork."

"What in particular?"

"I took in a girl and her baby. They were living in a box behind our neighborhood."

"Oh no, that's difficult to hear."

"Tell me about it. She's just sixteen, and her pregnancy didn't go over well with her foster father."

"I see. Let me make a call tomorrow, I'll let you know. What else do you have?"

Cradling Abby, Dawn came into the kitchen. "I'm sorry. But where do you keep the toilet paper?"

I stuck up a finger. "Hey, Ray, I've got to get off, but I wanted to tell you, your son, Tommy, helped me again."

"Good to hear. He's a good boy."

"He sure is. I'll talk to you later."

As I hung up, Dawn pleaded, "I'm sorry to bother you, but I really have to go."

"No problem. Hang on a second."

I jogged to the garage, grabbed two rolls of toilet paper, and came back into the house.

Handing them off, I said, "Let me take her so you can, you know . . ."

She gave me Abby and dashed down the hallway. As soon as the bathroom door closed, Abby started fussing.

Cradling her in my arms, I said, "Shhh, little one, Mommy will be right back."

I circled inside the house four times, and she finally quieted down. I was staring out the back slider when the doorbell rang.

Shifting Abby to my left arm, I opened the door.

Mario was holding an umbrella over his head. He looked at Abby and said, "Holy shit. What's going on?"

"Come in."

I stepped to the side, and Mario closed the umbrella and the door behind him.

"What's going on, bro? Don't tell me you're a secret daddy or something."

Dawn came into the room, and Mario whispered, "Oh my God. She looks like Bev."

I said, "I know. Right?"

I gave Abby back to Dawn, saying, "Dawn, this is the foster brother I mentioned, Mario. Mario, meet Dawn and her baby, Abby."

"Nice to meet you. So, how do you know each other?"

I said, "I'll fill you in later."

Dawn sniffed Abby twice and said, "She needs to be changed."

"Oh, I didn't realize. I'm not used to this."

Mario laughed. "Do you even know how to change a diaper?"

Dawn said, "Nice to meet you, Mario. We're going in for the night."

Mario looked at me.

"Sleep good. If you need anything, let me know."

As soon as the spare bedroom door closed, Mario said, "She's hot, bro. The baby isn't yours, is it?"

Glaring at him, I said, "No, and Dawn is a just kid."

"What is she doing here."

I told him how Toby found them, and he said, "Man, we know what that's like."

"We sure do. I'm going to see what help I can get for her."

"How long is she staying here?"

"I don't know, but Laura isn't happy about it."

"I can't blame her, she's the real deal."

"She's not even seventeen, Mario."

"Just playing, man. What did you want to show me?"

I pulled my phone out and stepped into the kitchen. "Larson's kid used some new AI tool to enhance the video from the Crane case. Check it out."

Mario held the phone and watched the video. "I can't remember what the father looks like, but this is miles clearer."

"It's definitely the father, Atlas Crane."

He handed back the phone. "So, we got ourselves a case?"

"Probably."

"Probably?"

"There's one more thing I want to look into before I greenlight it."

"How much is this one paying?"

"It's not about the money."

"Everything is about the money."

"No, it's not. It's about evening the score, getting justice—"

"Justice doesn't pay the bills, bro."

"You complaining? You live across the street from the beach and have everything you need, right?"

"You know what I mean."

"Don't ever forget we came from nothing."

"Okay, Daddy."

"You know, people think once they're happy they'll be thankful, but they got it backwards; being grateful is the key to happiness."

"You and the stoic stuff."

"People like Seneca and Marcus Aurelius knew what they were talking about. Instead of discounting them, you should read what they said. They figured out a lot of stuff centuries ago."

"Yeah, yeah, yeah. You said you had something you wanted me to check out."

"You've got a friend, I think his name is Harvey or something."

"You mean Howie? The guy with the house on the bay?"

"That's him. He's got a nice boat, right?"

"Yeah, like a thirty-something-footer, it's the same as the one Vladmir has."

"Vladimir?"

"Igor, the Russian's right-hand man."

"Oh, right."

"Remember we saw his boat when we went to the marina to pick up the docs they made for the Cruz job?"

"Yeah, I do. It's off Bayshore Drive."

"Good, I was starting to worry about you, you know, early onset."

"So, about your friend Howie? We're going to need to borrow his boat. Can you arrange it?"

"What for?"

"Don't worry about why right now. Just go see him. Tell him we'll pay two thousand a day."

"How long and when?"

"I don't know, but not more than a day here and there, nothing on consecutive days."

12

———

I PUT A WARM BAG OF BAGELS ON THE KITCHEN COUNTER AND turned the coffee machine on. Tiptoeing down the hallway, I stopped in front of the guest room. No sounds were coming from the bedroom Dawn and Abby were calling home.

When she had gotten up during the night, I worried she was going to take off, but Abby was hungry, and Dawn was just looking for baby food.

It was 8:10 a.m. After making a cup of coffee for myself, I gently knocked on her door. "Dawn? Are you guys up?"

"Uh, yeah. We'll be out in a minute."

Ten minutes later they came into the kitchen.

"Did you sleep okay?"

She nodded. "It was the best one in a while."

"You see, you need a real bed."

"Thanks for letting us sleep here."

"No problem. Make yourself some coffee, and I got some bagels."

"Do you have any Coke? Or Pepsi?"

"No. That's not the best thing to be drinking."

She shrugged.

Pointing at the fridge, I said, "I have some sparkling waters, some are flavored if you're interested."

"I'm going to heat up some milk for Abby."

I opened my laptop. "Last night I checked some of the county sites that handle assistance. I've got a friend checking on speeding things up, but either way, we need to fill out some forms to get things started."

"Okay."

After putting Abby's bottle in the microwave, she stuffed a piece of bagel in her mouth. "These are good."

"While you guys eat, I'll get started filling the forms out."

"Okay."

"Is Dawn your first name?"

"Yeah."

"Last name?"

"Rothshield."

I stiffened. "Rothshield?"

"Yeah, that's right."

"How do you spell it?"

"R-O-T-H-S-H-I-E-L-D."

Curious about how common the last name was, I asked, "Do you know your Social Security number?"

She rattled it off.

"How about your biological parents?"

"I never met my father, but my mother's name is Beverly."

My heartbeat sped up. "Did they call her Bev?"

"Uh-huh, they did."

I stood. "Where are you from originally?"

"New Jersey."

My knees weakened. "Where in New Jersey?"

"I don't remember."

"Monmouth County?"

"Maybe, it sounds familiar, why?"

"Remember I said you looked like a girl I knew?"

"Yeah, so?"

"This is crazy, but maybe there's a chance you're her daughter."

"What?"

"Hold on a second."

I ran into my bedroom and returned with a tattered picture I dug out of my nightstand drawer.

"Look at this. I mean, she was only like ten years old at the time, but see how much you look like her?"

She held the picture close to her face. "Yeah. I do. That would be unbelievable if she was my mother."

"When was the last time you saw her?"

"I don't know, about when I was seven or eight. She had a bad problem with drugs, and they took me away from her. She tried to get clean, but she just couldn't do it."

"Did that happen in New Jersey?"

Her face darkened. "Yeah."

"I'm sorry. I know it's tough."

"I hardly ever saw her, and then I heard she moved away because she was sick."

"What kind of illness?"

"Something to do with the cold, and I guess since she was homeless it really affected her."

"Maybe it was Raynaud's Disease. It affects the blood flow to your extremities."

"Nobody ever said what it was, but I was just a kid."

"Did they say where she went?"

"Just that she went down south. I think she tried to get me, but the foster family did everything they could to keep her away from me."

"You never heard from her?"

"She sent me a letter saying it would be better to break all ties, said she was sorry she wasn't a better mother, but she was sick."

"That's terrible."

"I got over it."

"You never do, or at least I never did when my mother was killed."

"I'm just trying to survive, and there ain't no time to think about it."

Fingering the picture of Bev, I said, "I understand. You know, if you want, it might be possible to track her down."

"I don't know. But how would you do that?"

"I've got good contacts. I'm not saying it'd be easy or that we'd find her, but if you want, we can try."

She frowned. "I wonder where she is and if she's all right."

"Think about it. Now, let's get back to the paperwork."

With me helping, it took twenty minutes to complete the forms required. How would someone in need, without internet access, do it?

Dawn retreated to the bedroom to put Abby down for a nap, and I went onto the lanai. I called Mario.

"Hey, you're never going to believe it."

"What? You're dumping Laura for Dawn?"

I exhaled. "You know, sometimes you can be a jerk."

"I'm just busting, man. What's going on?"

"Her mother might be Bev."

"Our Bev?"

"Yep."

"No way."

"Her last name is Rothshield, and she's from New Jersey."

"It's probably a coincidence."

"I showed her that picture of Bev."

"What picture?"

"The one where she is sitting on the green couch the Maple Street house had."

"I can't believe you still have that."

"Dawn looks just like her."

"Really?"

"And she said they called her mother Bev."

"This sounds wild."

"You know, I always wanted to find Bev."

"You always felt bad leaving her behind when we ran away."

"We couldn't take her; she was just ten. We had no idea where we were going or what would happen and—"

"Hey, man, you don't need to make excuses. We had no choice."

"But now we do."

"What do you mean?"

"We can either look for Bev or not."

"You want to try?"

"A hundred percent. Dawn said she was using drugs and was homeless. We might be able to help her."

"But we don't know anything about where she is and even if she's still alive."

"We'll find out."

"It sounds impossible."

"It's not impossible, it's just difficult."

"Crazy difficult."

"As Seneca said, 'How does it help by making troubles heavier by complaining about them?'"

I visualized Mario rolling his eyes and said, "Look, we can do it, and we should. It's the right thing to do. We owe it to Bev."

13

GETTING OUT OF MY CAR, I WONDERED IF THE MURDERED woman had an attraction to men who liked being on the water.

I walked down a dock where an imposing tugboat was tied up. Water lapped against the rust-stained hull of the vessel named *Coastal Fort Myers*. I was there to see Fred Foster.

Two men in rubbery overalls were smoking on the deck of the boat. One of them had been the boyfriend of Ana Crane when she was murdered.

"Fred!"

He looked up. "Jeffrey?"

I had given the former vitamin store owner an alias, telling him I was a journalist. "Yeah."

"Hold on." He said something to his mate and scampered down a gangplank.

He stuck out a meaty hand. "How are you doing?"

"Good. Thanks for meeting with me."

"Of course. You said it was about Ana. Even though it's been years, I'm still sick about what happened."

"I know you testified at the trial, but I wanted to ask you about Atlas Crane."

He frowned. "The bastard got away with murder."

"What can you tell me about him?"

"He's a lying coward. You know, he has a history of violence. He's a nasty man. I tried to protect her from him after she told me he'd hit her. I wouldn't let him into the house when he came to pick up Tyler."

"He got physical with her?"

"Yeah, she said he shoved her into the kitchen island and said she had a gigantic bruise on her hip."

"Did she report it?"

"No. But I told her to get a restraining order on him. He wasn't happy to see me with her. The guy was like a pot of water on the verge of boiling. I've worked with a lot a guys like him. They lose their temper, just like that." He snapped his fingers.

"She never went for the restraining order?"

He wagged his head. "Believe it or not, she said if she did it would make him angry, and she was afraid she'd set him off. I told her that was exactly why she needed it. Ana was a great girl. She wanted Tyler to have a relationship with his father."

"Did you get along with Tyler?"

"Oh yeah. He's a good kid. I mean, we keep in touch, but when Ana was, uh, killed, Tyler stuck up for his father. I get it, he was just ten years old or so, but things were a bit strained. I'm sure that bastard was whispering in Tyler's ear about me."

"Do you know if Tyler and his father get along these days?"

"Not really."

"Is there anything else you can tell me about Atlas Crane?"

"Just that he should be behind bars for the rest of his life."

"I appreciate your time."

"Why are you asking about all this now?"

"I'm writing a piece on unsolved murders in Southwest Florida."

"Really?"

"Yeah, you'd be surprised how many there are. Take a guess."

"Fifty?"

"No, over four hundred."

"Wow."

"I'm trying to shed some light on them."

"That'd be good."

"I hope so. Hey, how long are you doing this?"

"Right after Ana was killed, I sold the vitamin shop I had. It was doing okay, but I had to change things up, you know."

"I get it. I didn't know there were tugboats in Fort Myers. What do you guys do with the tugboat around here?"

"We do a lot. You know, we have a ton of narrow channels here, and we help some boats navigate them, and we do a lot of work placing and retrieving barges."

"Makes sense."

"Yeah, and of course if a boat is disabled, we can tow it in. Plus, we did a lot of salvage operations after Ian hit."

"I can imagine."

"Yeah, I worked twenty-nine days in a row."

"Wow. Thanks, for meeting with me."***

Driving back on Route 75, I cycled ideas, putting a mental pin in a bold one.

I took the alleyway running alongside M Waterfront and looked to the right. Tyler Crane was sitting on a bench overlooking Venetian Bay.

A lone boater was making his way to the Gulf. I cleared my throat to avoid startling Tyler and slid next to him.

He smiled and said, "I haven't been here in years. My mom used to take me here. We used to toss bread into the water and the fish would go nuts."

"This bay is loaded with fish. The catfish go for the bread."

"Yeah, I remember the first time seeing they had whiskers. They'd rush to the surface and thrash about going for the bread. It was fun."

"I'm sure it was."

"So, did you look into my fath—"

I put a finger to my lips, and he said, "Sorry, sorry."

Lowering my voice, I said, "Did you ever think about going after him civilly? Double jeopardy doesn't apply to civil suits."

He whispered, "He's broke. He wasn't a saver to begin with, and he spent whatever he had on the lawyers who got him off. Besides, that's not what I'm after, I want justice for my mom."

"And what does that look like to you?"

"He's got to go to prison."

"Let's take a walk."

We headed toward the parking lot. Kids were running through alternating spouts of water shooting into the air. I leaned into Tyler.

"How are you getting along with him these days?"

"The same as always."

"He doesn't suspect that you believe he killed your mother?"

"No, he's clueless and goes on like nothing happened."

"I have a couple of ideas. But I have to warn you, they're rough."

"You mean violent?"

"No. But this is going to get as dirty as it gets. I have to know if you're up to it or not."

"I understand."

"I need more than understanding. I need your buy-in and help if I need it."

His eyes widened but he said nothing.

"Are you all the way in or not?"

He nodded. "He needs to pay for what he did. I'm in."

I looked him straight in the eye. "There's no turning back on this, you know?"

"I understand. Let's do it. The sooner the better."

"Okay. I hope you're a good poker player."

"What do you mean by that?"

"You have to maintain good relations with your father. Keep things normal. He can't know anything might be going on."

"No problem. I never said how I really felt about everything. I supported him as best as I could, even though doubts started creeping in. Make that flooding in."

"You have to stay on good terms with him."

"I will, no worries."

"There's going to be expenses and fees that have to be paid."

He nodded. "Mr. Larson told me about them. Don't worry, I've got the money from selling the house Mom left me."

"Okay. I'll discount our end a little, but the expenses are what they are."

"Sounds good."

"And remember, unless there's a real emergency, don't reach out. When and if I need you, I'll be in touch."

As he said, "No problem." I turned and headed for the tunnel that led to the other side of Venetian Village.

14

—————

TURNING INTO PELICAN MARSH, I NAVIGATED TO THE ARBORS neighborhood. Larson was in the driveway inspecting a wide border of purple and white flowers lining the landscape beds.

I said, "It looks good."

"I liked the begonias, but they were getting ratty."

"You're really on top of this place. It looks amazing."

"Thanks."

I followed him around the side of the house onto the lanai. A golfer was ready to swing, and we stood still until he made contact with the ball. I tried to follow its flight but never seemed able to do it.

Larson said, "That was a nice shot."

"It sounded like one."

He plopped onto a club chair. "I heard from Vincent on the girl who is staying with you."

"Is he going to help?"

Larson nodded. "They approved the application, and she should be able to move into a house today."

"That's great. What kind of house?"

"It'll be a shared home."

"A group home?"

"Yes. He said St. Matthew's House has a slot in Campbell Lodge that she can have."

"Dawn has an infant daughter."

"I'm aware, and so are they. This is transitional housing."

"I don't know about this."

"I'm surprised to hear that." Larson chuckled. "What were you expecting, a condo on the beach?"

"I'm just worried about her, that's all. I know what these places are like, and she's a good kid. I don't want her to get off track."

Larson took his phone out. "I'm forwarding the email on the St. Matthew's House housing."

"Thanks."

He pocketed his cell and said, "So, Laura's not too pleased with you taking in Dawn and her child."

"What makes you say that?"

Larson smiled. "I can tell."

"Everything is cool with her."

"Come on, Beck. I know something's going on. You know you can confide in me, I might be able to help."

I filled him in on how Laura had reacted, including our argument over moving in together.

Lawson said, "Laura's acting normal. It seems like you're at a crossroads in the relationship, and she's taking the lead to move it to the next stage."

"Well, I don't think it's fair to push me."

"From the outside, she seems good for you."

"We get along great, it's just that I need my space, you know?"

"I understand, but you might be missing out on something a whole lot better. My marriage was the best thing that ever happened to me."

"Now you've got me married?"

"Well, if you move to the next step and it works, why not?"

I shrugged. "We'll see. Look, I didn't come her for relationship advice."

Larson said, "I'm only trying to help. So, what's on your mind?"

"I'm torn over an idea for the Atlas Crane case."

"How so?"

I gave Larson an overview of my plan.

He said, "I think it'll be effective."

"Me too, but I'm not sure it feels right."

Larson nodded slightly. "Your concerned over the morality'?"

I hadn't categorized what I was feeling, but it sounded correct. "I don't know what you'd call it, but don't you think it's pushing the envelope?"

"You have to consider the circumstances and the objective."

"I'm not sure what you mean."

"Would you agree that there isn't a worse crime than taking a life?"

"Yes, though human trafficking is right up there."

"Agreed, but with trafficking there is a chance for the victims to escape. Though scarred, they're alive and can attempt to overcome the damage and try to live a happy life."

"Sometimes they may be better off dead."

"True, but let's not get off track. The bottom line is this man killed his wife and got away with it. Right?"

"Yes."

"Therefore, whatever you do to get a measure of justice for his son isn't off limits."

"I guess so."

"No." Larson scooched to the edge of his seat and looked

me in the eye. "You have to believe it's justified, or your plan will not work."

I nodded but said nothing.

Larson said, "And even worse than the plan failing is you might get hurt in the process."

"I'm going to be fine."

"If you're not a thousand percent behind your plan, then toss it and start over."

"It's a good one, I think it's the only way to get the job done."

"Then get on board and kick the doubts out of your head."

I bounced out of Larson's house and sent a text to Mario: *The job is on.*

15

———

THE PURPLE INTERIOR THREW ME OFF. I'D NEVER BEEN TO THE Lavender Café & Bistro, but the bustle was a sign I'd been missing something.

Detective Moreno was sitting at a table along the wall. I pulled a colorful chair out and sat. Moreno pointed to a small cup in front of him. "You ever try Turkish coffee?"

"No. It looks thick, like mud."

"It's a little sandy but good. Have a cup."

"Sure. Why not?"

"If you're hungry, they have a house specialty. It's three eggs that are slowly cooked in a sauce. It's so good."

I flagged down a server, saying, "I'll just have a coffee. A Turkish one."

Moreno said, "You've got another job?"

"Yes, but I wanted your help on something else."

"Shoot."

I filled him in on the background concerning my foster sister, Bev.

"Wow. I thought it was just you and Mario that were tight."

I exhaled. "It sucked having to leave her behind when we escaped. But she was just too young."

"And you never tried to find her?"

"Don't remind me. I've been on more guilt trips than vacations."

"Sorry, man."

The server brought my coffee. I took a sip. "It's strong. And gritty."

"Exactly."

I took another sip. "I like it though. I'll have to come back."

"If you do, try the Moroccan skewers. They're made with chicken, and it's my favorite."

"I'll check it out. Let me finish what I was saying."

I brought him up to date on finding Dawn and her kid in the woods.

He said, "You're a good man, Beck. It's not easy doing what you did. Everybody likes to say they'd help someone, but when it comes down to it, people turn the other way. Believe me, what I see out there isn't pretty. You stepped up, and that's to be commended."

I found myself wishing Laura could hear what Moreno said. "I've been where she is, and I just had to help. You know, what I wanted to talk about is related."

"Tell me about it."

"In the last foster home Mario and I were in, the foster father was abusive." I fingered the scar behind my ear. "It's how I got this."

"I remember you saying it's what made you and Mario take off."

"Yeah, but when we ran, we left Bev behind. She wanted to come, but she was way too young and—"

"And now you want to find her?"

"How'd you know?"

He smiled. "I'm a detective, pal."

Returning the smile, I said, "Do you think you could get some information for me? You know, point me in the right direction?"

"What state was she last in?"

"I don't know. But for sure she was in New Jersey. In Monmouth County."

He took a notebook out. "What's her name and approximate age?"

I rattled it off.

"Let me check what the system may have on her. I'll see if the DMV up there has anything. She might have a record or encounter of some kind that could make it easier to trace her."

"I don't think she was doing too well. I think she might have been using, and that led to her walking away from her daughter."

Moreno sighed. "You sure you want to dig into this? It might get nasty."

"I have to."

"I understand."

"Thanks, I owe you."

"Friends don't keep score."

My cell buzzed. It was Mario.

"Hey, what's going on?"

He asked, "Where are you?"

"On Vanderbilt Beach Road heading home."

"I've been watching Atlas Crane to get his routine down, like you said."

"Okay."

"I just followed Crane to the Naples City Dock. I'm sure he's about to go fishing."

"Is he alone?"

"Yep."

"Can we get your buddy's boat?"

"I asked him before I called you. He's cool with it."

"Perfect."

"He lives in Royal Harbor. I'm five minutes away. I'll drop you a pin."

"I'll see you there."

After parking, I pulled off my sneakers and grabbed a pair of flip-flops from the trunk. Cutting between houses, I saw Mario sitting behind the wheel of his friend's Boston Whaler.

I called out to him and hopped onto the twenty-eight-footer. I ducked into the shade the hardtop provided.

Pointing to the pair of rods standing at the rear of the boat, I said, "Nice touch."

"I figured they'd look good."

"Let's get going."

Mario fired up the motors, and I threw the lines onto the dock. Pulling up one of the bumpers, I said, "Do you know where he usually likes to fish?"

"Yeah, he has two spots, and they must be good because there's always a couple of other boats in both areas."

Mario navigated toward the bay, keeping the boat's wake to a minimum. After passing the end of the no-wake zone, Mario pushed the throttle forward. The front of the boat lifted.

The bay widened and he steered toward the north end.

I stepped toward the front. Tugging my baseball cap lower, I asked, "Did you bring any sunscreen?"

"Nah. I hate putting that stuff on."

I ducked back under the shade. "You have to be careful. The Florida sun is intense."

Slowing down, he thrust a chin. "That's Crane, to the right."

There was a cluster of boats. "Which one?"

"The blue one."

Squinting, I focused on a boat with a broad blue band around its hull. "Get close but not too close."

Mario slowed down. I waved to a couple of boats as we approached the area where Atlas Crane was fishing.

As we got within earshot of Crane's boat, Mario cut the engine.

I grabbed a fishing rod.

Raising my voice, I said, "Where's the bait?"

Mario said, "You were supposed to get it."

"No, I wasn't. I told you to get it!"

"No way, man! You said you were getting it."

Crane was looking in our direction when I shouted, "I did not!"

As our boat drifted closer to Crane's, I said, "You're losing it, man!"

"It's not my fault."

"It is! I told you I had no time today. What now? We've got to go back?"

Mario said, "What do you want me to do?"

"Bring the damn bait! I ask you to do one thing and you blow it. I can't believe it."

"Sorry, man."

"Let's get the hell out of here."

"Hold on a second." Mario went to the side of the boat and waved his arm, "Hey! Yo! Is there any way we can borrow some bait?"

I said, "You can't borrow bait, dummy. If he can help us, we'll pay for it."

Atlas Crane stood and put his rod into a holder. He cupped his hands around his mouth "You need bait?"

"Yeah, we forgot to get some."

I pointed at Mario, "I didn't forget, he did."

Crane hesitated before saying, "Sure, I can spare some."

"Thanks, man, you're a lifesaver."

"Come a little closer."

Mario started the engine. I threw the bumpers over the side, and we slowly moved toward Crane's boat. When we were a yard away, Crane threw a line, and I snagged it. We pulled each other together.

I held out a fifty. "We appreciate it. Here's something for you."

Crane snatched it like it was the Hope Diamond. He pocketed it, saying, "Fifty is way too much."

"Nah, it's fine. I only have a little time. Otherwise coming out here was a waste. Mario, get the bucket."

Crane took the bucket and dumped a scoop of bait in it.

I said, "How's the fishing?"

"Pretty good—caught a couple of snook, and I just started."

"Nice. I'm new to the area, and it's the first time out for me."

"You fish regularly?"

"I just moved down here and got into fishing about a year ago."

"That's a nice boat."

"It's Mario's. I've got a boat of my own, a fifty-footer with radar and all."

"Wow. That's sweet."

"I really like being out on the water."

"Yeah, it's peaceful out here."

"I know what you mean. Sometimes I just go out without even dropping a line. A hundred yards from the shore, you feel like you're on a different planet."

Crane said, "That's so true. Where do you dock your boat?"

"I just bought it and I'm keeping it at a friend's house. He has a dock with a huge boatlift."

"I guess the price is right."

"Where do you think I should dock it?"

"I've been using Naples City Dock. They're reasonable. They dock boats up to sixty feet."

"Good to know. Like I say, mine is a fifty-footer. It's a Cabo Flybridge, perfect for fishing."

"That's a gem of a boat. I've never been on one, but some guy used to have one two docks away from mine."

"Well, you have to come out on mine sometime."

"That'd be great. Oh, by the way, my name is Atlas. Atlas Crane."

"Nice to meet you. I'm Beck, and this is Mario."

"Say, since you're a newbie, you should come down to the Naples Fishing Club. It's a good place to meet people. We have a meeting once a month, on the third Tuesday of every month at six thirty. You can come for free and see if it's for you."

"That's a great idea. I'll check it out. All right, we'll get out of your hair. Thanks again for the bait."

Mario started the engine, and we pulled away from Crane's boat. When we were a city block away, Mario said, "He bought that hook, line, and sinker."

I smiled.

"That was a pretty good line, no?"

"It was witty. But don't celebrate, the hard parts are coming."

16

———

Laura wasn't responding to my texts. I called her.
"Hey, how is it going?'

"Fine."

Fine and good were close in meaning, except when spoken by a woman. "What are you doing?"

"Why?"

"I wanted to see if you wanted to take a ride."

"Where?"

I was betting the streak of one-word answers was about to break. "Larson arranged for a place for Dawn and Abby to live."

"He did?"

Two was better than one. "Yep. Nobody has the connections he has. So, you want to go?"

"You're taking her there?"

"Not yet. I wanted to see the administrator and the place first, but it's a done deal."

"You want me to drive over to your place?"

"No. I'll pick you up, it's on the way."

Laura was waiting outside when I pulled up. She hopped into the passenger seat and leaned over, planting a kiss on my cheek. The news that Dawn and her baby were leaving had thawed the freeze.

Buckling her seat belt, she said, "How far do we have to go?"

"It's not far, off Collier Boulevard and Vanderbilt."

"Good. I was just talking to Susan. She said her and Mario are going to see a Pink Floyd cover band. You want to go with them? It'll be fun."

"If you want to, sure."

"Good. I'll tell her to get us tickets. You want to grab something before the show?"

"Okay."

"Is everything all right?"

"Yeah, why?"

"You're giving me one-word answers."

I wanted to tell her I was still trying to process her jealousy, but said, "I didn't realize it. I guess I'm a little distracted thinking about this new case we have."

"What kind of a case is it?"

"I can't really talk about it."

"That's ridiculous. We're going out for years and you told me about—"

"It concerns a man who might have murdered his wife."

She put her hand over her mouth. "Oh my God. That's disgusting."

I nodded.

"Why isn't he going to jail?"

"He was found not guilty."

"But you think he did it?"

Her detective skills were good. "It looks that way."

"What are you going to do?"

"I'm not sure yet. That's why I was thinking about it."

"If he did it, why can't the police do something?"

I explained double jeopardy to her.

"That's crazy. Are you saying if new evidence is discovered, someone can't be put on trial again?"

"That's the law."

"How can that be?"

I turned into the driveway leading to a two-story rectangular building. "We're here."

She said, "This is the place Dawn is going to live?"

"Yes."

"It looks like a run-down motel."

Several people were hanging out on the exterior corridor that ran along the top floor. "It's just a temporary thing."

She pointed to a long section of railing covered with clothing. "With this humidity, there's no way that laundry is going to dry."

We parked and got out of the car. Three different sources of music competed for your attention. A shirtless boy was bouncing a soccer ball off his knee near a scuffed door marked Office.

The closer we got to the building the more peeling paint we saw. Two women were sitting to the right of the office door, conversing in Spanish.

I knocked on the door and a slender woman opened up. "Yes?"

"Hey, I'm Beck. Ray Larson said you have a place for Dawn and her baby."

Her eyes scanned Laura from head to toe. "Okay, but if she's looking for a Hilton, this ain't it."

"We understand. Mr. Larson said you'd show us around."

"What are you, her guardian or something?"

Laura said, "No. We just have her best interests at heart"

She nodded. "All right. Let's go, I don't have a ton of time."

We stepped into a small space. A fan was blowing papers off a metal desk. We walked down a dark hallway into a kitchen. Two picnic tables were filled with women and their children. All eyes were on us. It was hard to hear my own thoughts.

I nodded to them as we walked past countertops filled with bulk packages of cereal, canned foods, and paper goods.

We followed her into another room where a TV was blaring. "This is the rec room."

Half a dozen kids were glued to a cartoon show, and a toddler was banging a toy nonstop. My gaze went to several stains on the rug.

Laura scrunched her nose, whispering, "What's that smell?"

The air was heavy and musty. "It's probably mildew."

"It better not be mold."

"You want to see the laundry?"

"No thanks. Can we have a peek at her room?"

"Down here."

A mother yelling at her kid passed us in the hallway. Our guide pointed to a door. "She'll be rooming with Luiza."

She threw open the door. To the right, an unmade bed and crib were surrounded by cardboard boxes. Opposite that was a bare mattress and a marred nightstand.

"Dawn has an infant daughter."

"Yeah, we know."

Laura said, "This the best you have for her?"

"Lady, this ain't no hotel."

Laura looked at me and said, "Okay. Thanks for the tour."

As soon as we hit the parking lot, Laura said, "We can't let them live here."

I stopped short. "It's not the best, but what else can we do?"

"Can't you let her stay at your place until something better is available?"

Was this Laura talking? "I guess so, but I think most of these places are going to be group homes."

"I can't imagine a mother and her baby living in a place like that."

Laura, luckily, hadn't seen what I had. "It's what it is. You do what you have to do."

"Maybe we can find her a short-term rental until she gets on her feet. I can pitch in a couple of hundred a month."

I grabbed her hand and kissed it. "That's nice, but it's unnecessary. I can afford to do it for a while."

"You're a good person."

I wasn't sure of that. "If I am, it's because I'm hanging around with you."

She flashed her thousand-watt smile. "See? We make a good team."

I smiled and opened the car door for her. Starting the car, I said, "Do you want to check on the rental market? We can probably do with a one-bedroom."

She had her phone in her hand. "I'm on Zillow."

"If you find something, we can see if they're open to a short-term rental. If we have to pay more, I'm cool with it."

"How is she going to get on her feet and pay her own way with a baby? Do you know how much childcare costs?"

I didn't. "We have to figure something out. Worst comes to worst, I can pay for the childcare when she gets her own place. It's got to be less than paying rent."

"She'd need a job."

"I know. Look, I know it's a shot in the dark, but I'm trying to track down her mother."

"And what do you think she's going to do? She abandoned her. You expect her to come to the rescue?"

I hadn't really thought much about it. "I don't know what's she'll do. But first, we have to find her. And it's not going to be easy."

"I know you're trying to do the right thing, but it can easily backfire."

17

I kissed Laura's cheek and said, "You did a great job finding an apartment for Dawn."

"Thanks, but if you weren't willing to pay for it . . ." Her voice trailed off.

Paying over two thousand dollars a month wasn't cheap, but Dawn and her baby would be safe, and I'd removed a flashpoint from my relationship with Laura.

"It's not forever. Please try to keep an eye on her with that virtual typing class."

"She's doing good. I think if she keeps at it for a week, she'll be typing at a quick enough pace."

"Larson said there are a couple of accounting outfits with data entry jobs in town. She can do it from the apartment and make some money."

"How much do they pay?"

"Sixteen an hour."

"That's not going to go far. They have to eat, and she needs to get a car and—"

"One step at a time."

Laura lowered her voice. "She doesn't know how to cook."

"She had no one to learn from. She's just a kid."

"That's a shame. Are you going to teach her to cook?"

"Me?"

She poked my ribs. "You're always bragging about how good a chef you are."

I pulled her into me. "She's got to start at the bottom. My level of culinary artistry is too sophisticated."

"Okay, Mr. Michelin Star, don't get a big head."

Nuzzling her neck, I said, "Something else is getting big."

She broke my embrace. "Not now. I promised to take Dawn and Abby to the park."

"Aw, come on, that's not fair."

"I thought you and Mario were going to the boat club."

"It's a fishing club, but that's tonight."

"While you're there, I'll teach Dawn some of the basics of cooking."

I put a pout on. "But what about me?"

She smiled. "I'll come back later, don't worry."

The lot for the VFW hall was half empty. Mario pulled into a spot, and we got out.

A black awning covered the entrance to the bland, one-story building.

It was dark in the main room. Four men were drinking at a bar that ran along a wall. We walked past the bathrooms into a hallway that led to a large, square room filled with banquet tables.

A stack of newsletters sat on a table. I picked up a copy of *The Hook*, the club's publication, and leafed through it.

Mario whispered, "He's here, talking to an old guy by the window."

I waved to Atlas Crane and we sauntered over.

Crane said, "Hey, you made it."

"Of course. Thanks for inviting us."

He interrupted a group and introduced us to a couple of the members, who weren't friendly.

Crane said, "The meeting's going to get started in a second." He smiled. "There isn't anything that important. Except a contest that's coming up with some nice prize money."

"Cool."

A white-haired man banged on a tabletop. "Let's get this underway."

Crane said, "Come with me."

We followed him to someone who turned out to be the club president, and introduced us.

After thanking us for attending, he shouted, "The meeting is called to order."

The men who'd been at the bar came into the room and everyone took chairs.

The club president spoke about a snook-fishing contest, charter boat information, and a new initiative called Buddies Without Boats. The meeting was quickly adjourned.

Crane said, "That wasn't too painful, was it?"

"Not at all. It's nice and easygoing."

"Just like fishing."

"Yeah."

"Let's get a drink."

Crane said hello to the man tending bar, but the bartender didn't return the greeting, saying, "What do you want?"

We ordered beers on tap. The bartender put them on the bar, and Crane grabbed one. He turned his back, leaving me to pay for the drinks.

Crane raised his glass. "A bad day fishing is still better than a good day working."

I caught Mario rolling his eyes, but then he clicked Crane's glass. "Amen."

"So, you think you're going to join?"

"Sure, why not? I mean, it's just a hundred bucks."

"Yeah, and you always got somebody to go fishing with if you need them."

"Sounds good to me."

"Did you make arrangements where to dock your boat?"

"Not yet. It's still at my buddy's place. Man, wouldn't it be nice to have a dock right outside your house?"

"You're talking crazy money. What's your friend do?"

"He inherited it from an uncle who never had kids."

"That's one lucky bastard."

"You should see this house. I mean, it's old and was built before everything went crazy down here, but the views, they're incredible."

"Where is it at?"

"Devil's Blight in Park Shore."

"I don't know it, but I dig the name."

"Say, that fishing contest sounds like fun."

"This one is a good one. They got Yamaha to sponsor it, and the top prize is freaking twenty-five hundred bucks."

"That's nice. They said it was family friendly. Maybe I'll bring a woman friend of mine. She's not my girlfriend, we're just friends. You have any family?"

"Just a son."

"Why don't you ask him to come and we'll go out on my boat. I've got radar and all, and it may not be fair, but I'm willing to bet we'll bag the winner."

"That'd be nice, I can use the dough."

"Then let's do it. If we win, the prize money is yours. Check with your son. It'll be fun, and I can use some fishing lessons anyway."

Crane didn't spit out the usual. *"Oh, I couldn't do that, it wouldn't be fair.* Or even, *Let's see if we even win first."* Instead, he said, "I'll check with Tyler, my son, and let you know, but even if he doesn't want to go, count me in."

"That's cool. What's your number, I'll text you a pin."

He rattled it off and pulled out an iPhone, "Give me yours, in case there's a mix-up or something."

"That's the new Apple model?"

"Yeah. What a pain in the ass getting the apps and pass-words. I mean, why doesn't it just transfer everything?"

"You're right. But it syncs with your iPad?"

"Yeah, everything is up in the cloud, except when you need it."

We both laughed and I said, "I have to get going. I'll see you next week."

After starting the car and putting the air-conditioning on, I took a burner phone out of the glove box. Plugging a number in, I eased out of the parking lot.

Tyler answered on the second ring. "Hey, it's Beck."

"Oh, hi. What's going on?"

"Your father is going to ask you to go with him to a fishing contest. Tell him you'll go."

"Okay. When is it?"

"Next week."

"Why do you want me to go?"

"It's part of the plan."

"What do I have to do?"

I explained what he was to do.

"But why do you need me to do that?"

"That's all I can tell you at this point. You'll have to trust me. Okay?"

"All right."

"I have to run, another call is coming in."

I answered the call from Detective Moreno. "Hey, Mo. What's going on?"

"I got some information for you on the foster girl."

I tightened my grip on the wheel. "What do you have?"

"Where are you?"

"By Pine Ridge and Collier Boulevard."

"Meet me at Cracklin' Jack's."

A cartoony alligator anchored the sign for the eatery that billed itself as a taste of the Everglades. The parking lot for the red building was nearly full.

I stepped inside. It was noisy and harked back to a Florida long gone. Moreno was sitting at their wooden bar.

He patted my back. "You have to try the catfish here, it's the best. They fry it in the good old Southern way."

"I see you any more often and I'll need to go on a diet. How the hell do you eat all of that?"

"Moderation, my friend. My grandmother taught me to always leave something on your plate."

"A hell of lot safer than taking Ozempic."

The bartender came over.

Moreno said, "I'll have the fried chicken." He turned to me. "What are you having?"

"I ate already."

"Get something. Try the vittles or hush puppies."

"I'll go with the hush puppies."

The bartender left and I said, "So what do you have on Bev?"

"She left New Jersey. When, I can't say, but we know she was in Georgia and then Florida."

A surge of adrenaline coursed through me. "She's in Florida?"

"She could be, but her driver's license was never renewed, and that was six years ago."

"Where in Florida?"

"Her last known address was a halfway house in Orlando."

"A halfway home? For drugs?"

"She's been arrested for that, but this was for prostitution."

My heart sank to my toes. I raised my arm and called out to the bartender. "Can I have a Tito's on the rocks? Make it a double."

Moreno said, "I'm sorry this is messy."

"I never should have left without her."

"Come on, man. You said she was, what, ten years old?"

I nodded. "This is really screwed up."

The bartender put my drink down and I took a gulp.

Moreno patted my forearm. "Look, maybe you should just let this go."

"I can't. I just can't."

"Think it over."

"I've got to try to find her, give her a second chance."

"Don't take it the wrong way, but it's more like a seventh chance for her. She's been arrested two other times for soliciting, three for possession and—"

"I'm afraid to ask, but do we know if she's still alive?"

"Her social security number is still valid. It's not active, but it's not been canceled, not that that means anything these days."

"What was her last known address?"

He took his sport jacket off the back of the stool and dug into its breast pocket. "Here's a copy of her DMV record. Like I said, it expired six years ago, so the picture is about fourteen years old. But it has her last known address."

I studied the picture of Bev: mangy hair and a lined face. She was years younger than me but looked older. Resignation began creeping in. I blinked away a tear and concentrated on the slight smile she wore. She'd been such a sweet kid.

"You can only do so much, Beck."

"I have to do what I have to do."

18

—————

Laura pulled up before I had a chance to hit the button to close the garage door. I waited for her to come up the driveway.

Before she pecked my cheek, she said, "Are you all right?"

I opened the interior door, "Yeah, why?"

"On the phone you sounded down."

"I got some news about Bev."

"What's going on with her?"

"Who the hell knows? Moreno gave me this."

She took the DMV record. "I can see the resemblance to Dawn, but you said she was younger than you. It doesn't look like it."

"She's had a rough life."

"What did Detective Moreno say about her?"

"Six years ago she was living in a group home in Orlando. But he wasn't able to find anything after that."

"That's makes it easier if she's in Florida."

"I guess so."

"What do you mean? It's better than finding out she was in Texas or something. It'll be quicker to track her down."

"If she's still alive."

Her eyes widened. "You, you think she might be dead?"

"I don't know, but she was arrested several times for drugs and prostitution."

"Oh my God. That's so sad." She reached for my hand. "I'm sorry, Beck."

"What are you sorry about? It's not your fault."

"It's not yours either."

"I don't know about that."

"Well, I do."

"If I didn't leave her behind—"

"Stop it right there. She was just a kid, and you were barely sixteen." She stroked my hand. "Honey, you have to stop beating yourself up. It's not helping."

I shrugged.

"What you're doing for Dawn and trying to find Bev is amazing."

It was tempting to remind her she hadn't felt that way when I found Dawn and Abby sleeping in a box.

"I'm thinking of taking a ride up to Orlando, see what I can find out."

"I'll come with you."

"I'm not sure that's a good idea."

"Why not?"

"I've got a feeling it might get rough. Besides, I'm going to see a business associate there. He's got contacts and—"

She took a step back. "Fine. You want to do everything on your own, go for it."

"No, that's not it. In fact, I was going to ask you to help me with a job we just got."

She perked up. "The one where the husband killed his wife?"

"Yes, but please don't be repeating that."

"Sorry."

"All of our jobs are super confidential."

"My lips are sealed. So, what are you going to do?"

"Everything is on a need-to-know basis."

"What does that even mean?"

"At this point, keep Saturday free. I'll tell you more Friday, after I get back from Orlando."

I left before the first light of day and pulled into the lot for Unique FX at ten after ten. I sent a text, and two minutes later the door to the warehouse-type building popped open.

Tommy Larson smiled as I approached. "You made good time."

"Thank God it's offseason. It isn't as quiet as it used to be, but it's nice being able to get around easily."

"It's funny, when we first moved here, we dreaded the summer, but now it's our favorite time of the year."

I followed him into the cavernous space, asking, "The place is rocking. What are you working on?"

"The back half is finishing a big job on a paranormal film. It's taken us six months with all the changes to get it to the finish line." He pointed to a series of scaffolding. "And we just started on a new sci-fi series Universal Studios is doing."

"Nobody understands what it takes to put something realistic out these days."

"Computer graphics are a key tool, but you can't overdo it."

We stepped into his office. He opened the glass door to a refrigerator behind his desk. "You want something to drink?"

"I'm good."

Tommy twisted the cap off a bottle of Fiji water and said, "You said you needed help with something. If you need us to build something, we'd have to get on it before we start on a Disney project."

"Not this time."

"Is it about that video I enhanced for you?"

"No. I may need something on that, but not right now."

"The Hitchcockian suspense is killing me."

I told him about Bev.

"Wow. I know you and Mario were in foster care, but I didn't know you had a sister."

I sighed. "The truth is, I should've looked for her twenty years ago."

"Hey, man, all you got is the here and now. I'm telling you, you have to read the *Power of Now*, it'll help you stay in the present."

The past had rented a suite of rooms in my head. "I forgot about that book. I'll pick it up."

"Good. Now, how can I help you find her?"

"I remember, like two or three years back, you introduced me to a friend of yours. He was a documentary filmmaker."

"Chris Rotto, he's got one of those ZZ Top beards."

"Yeah, that's him."

"What about him?"

"At the time, he was making a documentary on drug houses in the Orlando area."

"It was a depressing film."

"From what I've been able to piece together, Bev was in Orlando, had a drug problem, and could've been homeless."

"You think she could be living in one of those drug dens?"

"It was several years ago, but someone might remember her. Can you ask him to bring me around to some of them?"

I hopped into Chris Rotto's pickup truck, and we drove to a run-down neighborhood on the outskirts of Orlando.

Rotto said, "This first one is the closest, geographically, to the address on your friend's license. I'm guessing you realize these places are transient, and the chances of finding someone who knows—"

"I understand, but you have to start somewhere."

Rotto made a left onto a street where the windows of most homes were boarded up. He pointed. "It's the one where the palm tree is down."

The roof was sagging, and the overgrown yard was littered with beer cans and fast-food wrappers.

Rotto knocked his knuckles on the front door and grabbed the doorknob. The door groaned as light flooded into a dark foyer.

"It's me, Rotto!"

We stepped inside. The linoleum flooring was filthy and curling away from what was left of the base moldings. I kicked aside a hypodermic needle and followed Rotto to the voices coming from the back.

Two girls in torn jeans were lying opposite each other on a stained, red velour couch. They were sharing a joint. Sprawled on a futon, a heavily tattooed man was talking on his phone. He eyed us and ended the call. He reached to his left and came up with a hunting knife.

"What do you want?"

"Take it easy. We're just looking for someone."

"And who would that be?"

Rotto showed him a picture, and the man said, "She ain't here."

"Okay. Thanks."

"What are you, narcos?"

"No. This girl is a friend, that's all. Mind if I ask the ladies?"

"Go ahead."

Neither of the girls gave any indication they recognized Bev. We'd just begun the search, but a futile feeling had started to settle in. I followed Rotto down a hallway.

Passing a doorless bathroom, the smell of urine burned my nostrils. We navigated around a pair of shopping carts filled with belongings to a room anchored by a dirty mattress. A pair of skinny addicts were laid out, mumbling to each other.

"Hey, you guys remember me?"

Only one of them picked his head up, staring vacantly at us.

Rotto held the picture in front of the drug user's glassy eyes. "Do any of you know this girl? Her name is Bev, she used to live around here."

The man shook his head as his friend nodded off, leaning into his buddy.

"Are you guys going to be okay?"

"Uh-huh."

"Make sure you eat something."

My stomach clenched as I followed Rotto toward the sound of someone grunting. He used the toe of his shoe to open a door to another bedroom. A sheet tacked to the ceiling separated two mattresses pitched on the floor.

I averted my eyes from a pair struggling to have sex on the bed to the left. Sitting on the edge of the mattress to the right was a shirtless man in his thirties. He was picking at a scab on his leg and didn't realize we were there.

Rotto said, "Hey, how's it going?"

His head lolled toward us. "Aw right."

"Can you take a look at this girl, see if you remember her?"

The man rubbed his eyes and took the picture from Rotto. My hopes soared as he brought it closer to his face.

"She looks like, I don't know her name or nothing, but, you know, maybe she's that one." He pointed to the sheet.

The parts of the woman I'd seen had no resemblance to Bev. I said, "Come on, let's go."

"Hey, can you guys spare some money? We gotta eat."

We turned to leave, but a man in a hoodie stepped in front of us. He held a gun near his waistline.

"Gimme your money! And jewelry."

Rotto said, "Take it easy. We're just looking for someone."

"Gimme the money. Now!"

I said, "Okay, man. We don't want no trouble."

"Hurry up." The man looked at Rotto's watch. "Gimme that watch."

Rotto started to take it off. I inched forward.

When Rotto handed over the watch, I pounced on the man. He fell backward. I jumped on his chest and pinned his arms back. "You pulled a gun on the wrong guy, pal."

Rotto said, "Are you all right?"

"Yeah. Grab your watch."

"Where's the gun?"

"It was a fake."

"Are you sure?"

"A hundred percent."

I dragged the mutt onto his feet. "Most guys you pulled that shit on would've busted you up. Now get the hell out of here."

Once we got back in the car, Rotto said, "How the hell did you know the gun wasn't real?"

"I wasn't completely sure, but it looked off, and he was using. I figured he would've hocked it if it was real. Besides, if it was real, I knew an addict's reflexes and strength would be easy to overwhelm."

"What if you were wrong?"

"You'd be driving me to the hospital instead of the next house. Let's go."

Rotto drove three short blocks, turning onto a street lined with small, cinder block homes. He pulled up to a yellow house. The red in the for sale sign had faded to pink.

In the gravel driveway sat a wheelless Ford Taurus on jacks.

My guide waved to a neighbor across the street who was mowing his grass. The man wagged his head and didn't return the greeting.

Rotto said, "Can you imagine living here?"

"No. It's got to be impossible to sell your house with one of these on your street."

"They're trapped."

"Why don't the cops do something about it?"

"I guess you didn't see my documentary. The police chase them out, sometimes securing the house, but the addicts move onto another empty property."

"Maybe they should be knocking some of these places down."

"We should be doing more to prevent addiction."

"Yes, and the first place is starting with supply. You do that, prices for that crap rise and put it out of touch for the younger kids."

"I don't know, it's about educating the kids, and"—Rotto turned his head toward an approaching van—"that's Robbie. He's a real angel."

"What's his story?"

"He's a recovering addict. Been clean for at least a decade, and he's dedicated his life to helping these people. He brings food and checks on them, sees if anyone needs medical attention."

The van pulled to a stop, and I followed Rotto over to it.

A man in his forties got out. He ran a hand through his thinning blond hair and smiled. "Hey, Rotto. Good to see you, man."

Rotto wrapped his arms around Robbie. "Good to see you, brother."

"Same here, man. What brings you around?"

Rotto introduced me and told him why we were here.

Robbie said, "I wouldn't give up on her, but it's a long shot. You got a picture of her?"

I showed him the DMV photo.

Robbie shook his head. "Wow. I actually remember her. It's been a long time, but she was at the place on Market Street before she got mixed up with the Albanians."

"What Albanians?"

"They're a gang run by this brutal bastard called Dren. He's into all kinds of crap, organized theft, prostitution, sex trafficking, you name something disgusting, Dren and his guys are behind it."

"How was Bev involved with them?"

"Dren knows this population is vulnerable and he uses them to profit. She was walking the streets for them."

My face flashed with heat. "Bastards."

"Eventually, they all do it. It's the only way they can earn the money they need for their habit."

"Where can I find this Dren character?"

Robbie said, "The Albanians are ruthless, but Dren is another level of nasty. I wouldn't be messing with them."

"I'm not messing with anybody. I just want to talk to them, see what they know about Bev."

Robbie turned to Rotto. "You remember what they did to the two girls who tried to escape from them? You wouldn't even put it in the film."

"You mean the trailer?"

"Yes. That was Dren, so I'd tell your friend to stay clear of them."

I said, "Don't worry about me. I can take care of myself, just tell me where I can find this Dren."

"As far as I know, he operates out of Pine Hills. But be fore-warned, it's a rough area, everyone calls it Crime Hills."

"Where exactly?"

"He's owns a pool hall and uses it to conduct business. It's called Nine Ball."

I turned to Rotto. "I'm going to head up there. You don't have to come, just bring me back to my car."

Rotto said, "Thanks, Robbie."

We got back in the car and Rotto said, "Look, these guys have no regard for life. I wouldn't fool with them."

"Like I said, you don't have to be involved. I got it from here."

Rotto pulled away from the curb. "Beck, I don't think it's a good idea to go it alone here. I'm a filmmaker, this is way out of my zone."

"It's okay. I appreciate everything you've done. I can take care of myself."

"Are you sure? You heard Robbie, these guys are dangerous."

"I got this, just get me to my car."

"Text me later. I want to be sure you're all right."

19

———

AFTER TAKING ANOTHER LOOK AT THE PICTURE OF DREN THAT Detective Moreno had texted me, I looked in the rearview mirror. The fake beard, glasses, and hat seemed convincing.

I got out of my car. There were half a dozen late-model cars in Nine Ball's parking lot.

Pulling open the door, I was assaulted by the smell of cigarettes and spilled beer. I squinted as my eyes adjusted.

The pool hall's dark interior was broken by a pattern of overhead lights hanging over two rows of pool tables.

Three of the green felt tables were being played by men with multiple tattoos.

Five men, holding drinks in front of the bar, turned in my direction. I gave a small nod, zeroing in on the one resembling Dren.

A player, bent over a table lining up a shot, straightened up as I passed. With a thick accent, he said, "What do you want?"

"Just a quick word with Dren. Nothing to worry about."

All the men except Dren put their drinks on the bar as I closed in. I raised both hands. "Just want a talk with Dren."

A refrigerator-sized man with a crooked nose stepped in front of his boss. "What are you doing here?"

"I'm looking for a girl."

"She ain't here."

"I can see that, my friend, but I want to show you a picture." I held up the DMV photo of Bev. "Her name is Bev."

"Like I said, she ain't here, so get the fuck out."

"I'm not looking for trouble. All I want is for Dren to take a look at the picture."

"You better leave or you're gonna be sorry."

I looked over the goon's shoulder. "Dren, I know you know her. She was working for you. I was paid to find out where she is."

"We don't know anything. Now get out!"

I stepped to the side, and looking at Dren, said, "I'm not asking you. I want Dren to tell me."

In a Slavic accent, Dren said, "Let him through."

"Thanks." I gave him the picture. "This is her. She worked for you."

His eyes betrayed him, and he quickly handed back the picture. "I don't know this one."

"Take another look."

"Time for you to go."

"Come on, tell me where she is."

Dren turned back toward the bar, saying, "Show him the way out."

I swung my left arm around his neck and with my right hand pulled my Glock out of the band of my pants. "Back off or your boss is dead!"

Dren's men pulled out guns and the pool players scurried out the door.

Dren remained calm. "You are making a big mistake. Let me go and we'll forget this all happened."

"Not until you tell me where Bev is."

"I told you, I don't know."

"I'm not buying that."

Dren's goons took a step closer. I pressed the barrel of the pistol into his cheek. "Tell your boys to back off. Now!"

"Back up!"

"Now, tell me where the girl is."

"I tell you already, I don't know where your bitch is."

I slammed the gun against the temple of his shaven head. "Where is she?"

"We sell her to Igor, the Russian."

I'd worked with a Russian named Igor several times. He had an operation producing counterfeit documents. "Who the hell is Igor?"

"He is a businessman, like me."

"What is he doing with Bev?"

"I don't know, ask him."

"Where is he?"

"I am not his father."

I squeezed my forearm into his windpipe. "Where is he?"

"He has bar on Mercy Drive."

"What's it called?"

It was the Igor I knew. "The Gator's Tail."

"You better be telling me the truth or I'll come back. I swear I will be back."

Dren laughed. "You are welcome, anytime."

I waved the gun at his men. "Put your weapons and car keys on the pool table."

They didn't make a move.

"Put them on the table!"

Dren nodded and his boys laid their firearms and keys on the pool table.

"Now, wait by the door."

I said to Dren, "Don't get any ideas."

I released him and kept my gun on him. With my free hand I knocked the guns onto the floor and kicked them toward a corner. I scooped up the car keys.

"You too, Dren, give me your car keys."

He handed them over and I said, "Turn around."

I poked Dren in the back with the barrel of my pistol. "Let's go."

As we walked to the door, I said, "Everybody outside."

Following Dren and his men outside, I said, "Keep walking and don't turn around until I say so."

I tossed all the car keys onto the roof of the bar.

Opening the door to my BMW, I shouted, "Keep walking."

Getting in the car, the unmistakable crack of a gunshot rang out.

I clutched my upper leg. Blood ran through my fingers.

I slunk down in the seat and started the car. Dren and his men were running toward me. I hit the gas and steered toward them.

20

———————

I parked in front of Lowdermilk Park and limped to Mario's condo.

His eyes bulged when he opened the door. "What the fuck happened?"

"I got shot in Orlando. It's not bad, Tommy Larson had a doctor look at it. Luckily it grazed the outside of my thigh."

"Holy shit! Who did this?"

I explained what happened.

"You never should've went there by yourself. That's crazy."

"I didn't think it would spin out of control. And I figured since I was up there—"

"You're something else. You're always preaching to me about being extra safe, and then you go do something like that."

"It was a mistake."

"The Albanians ain't going to forget about this, they'll come after you."

"I wore a disguise. All they know is I was looking for Bev, nothing more."

"What about your car?"

"I used an expired Texas plate and ditched it on the way back."

"You got lucky, man."

"And we got valuable information about Bev."

"If that Albanian isn't bullshitting you."

"I don't think he was. On the drive back, I checked, and it's the Igor we've worked with. I found out he was arrested once for human trafficking. The charges were dropped when the girls who made the charge refused to testify."

"He threatened them."

"For sure. We have to figure out how to deal with Igor."

"You know, a couple of weeks back, I heard some of his guys were grumbling, not happy with their cuts."

"Check around some, but first things first. We got the fishing contest in two days, so let's go over what we're going to do with Atlas Crane."

Sitting in the captain's chair of the boat owned by a friend of Larson's, Mario said, "You know, maybe I should get another boat."

I said, "Why? Look where we are? It's proof that having a friend with a boat is better than owning one."

"I kind of miss it."

"You didn't use it enough. If you're thinking about it, maybe you should join one of those boat clubs and use theirs to be sure."

"You have to reserve a boat in advance, but it's not a bad idea."

"Here comes Atlas and Tyler."

I stepped around the cabin and whispered to Laura, who was sunning herself. "They're here."

"How is your leg feeling?"

"It's okay."

"Good. You want me to meet them?"

"Not yet. Stay there and sun until I give you a thumbs-up."

Atlas looked at the yacht from the pier and said, "Man, this is some rig."

"Come aboard." They handed off their fishing rods and gear and got onto the boat.

I shook Atlas's hand. "What happened to your leg?"

"I gashed it."

"How the hell did you do that?"

"If you can believe it, I was on a ladder changing a high hat. I missed a step coming down and hit the corner of a table."

"Man, you gotta be careful with ladders."

"I know now."

He smiled and said, "This is my boy, Tyler."

Extending my hand, I said, "Glad to meet you. I'm Beck, and"—I pointed to my brother—"that's Mario."

Atlas said, "Who is that up front?"

"Laura, she's the friend of mine I mentioned."

"Is she your girlfriend?"

"No, we're just friends."

"You got some good-looking friends, Beck." He laughed.

"I'll introduce you later."

"She's got a hot body. I'd sure like to get some of that."

I wanted to throw him overboard but said, "Let's get out there and get our lines in the water."

Atlas said, "Yeah, I'm ready to win this thing!"

"Me too. Mario, let's get underway."

Tyler said, "Give me your phone and I'll take a picture of you before we head out."

Atlas handed over his cell.

"What's the PIN?"

"My birthday. I know I shouldn't, but I use it on everything."

Tyler took the picture and the boat lurched forward.

I said to Atlas and his son, "You can put your personal stuff down below; you don't want your phone getting dropped in the water."

Tyler turned to Atlas. "Great idea. Dad, give me your phone and wallet, I'll put them in the galley."

Atlas gave them to his son and said to me, "Did you get the bait I said to get?"

Pointing to two buckets in the shade, I said, "Yep, they're right there. I'm kind of lame at it, so I'm hoping you're good at baiting the hooks."

"Sure. I can do it with my eyes closed."

"Great. Check out the bait and make sure it's good, and I'll get Laura."

I looked at Tyler and nodded. He headed below as I called out, "Come here, Laura, I want you meet somebody."

"What? I can't hear you. The engine is too loud."

I elbowed Atlas. "Come on."

We held the railing and stepped toward where Laura was lying.

She put a winning smile on and stood up.

"Laura, this is Atlas."

She giggled. "Hi there, Atlas."

"Nice to meet you."

"Are you strong like the real Atlas?"

"Believe me, I'm as real as it gets."

She laughed. "I meant the Atlas in Greek mythology."

"Oh. He was that guy who holds up the world."

"Kind of. He sided with the Titans in their war against the Olympians, and when they lost, Zeus punished him, making him hold up the sky for eternity."

"I didn't know that story. You know your mythology."

"There's a lot of good stories there. I'd love to tell you some more."

"Sure, Teach, I'll take you up on the offer."

I said, "That will have to wait, we have a contest to win."

"He's right. It'll have to wait."

We left her, and Atlas whispered, "How old is she?"

"I don't know, maybe thirty-eight or so."

He nodded. "Man, what an ass on her. I'd like to hook up with her."

"She seemed to like you."

"You think so?"

"Definitely."

Tyler came on deck. His father said, "You were down there all this time?"

My stomach dropped.

The kid frowned. "I had to go number two."

His father slapped his son on the back. "You gotta go, you gotta go."

"Atlas, you want to go up to the bridge? You can check out the fish-finding gear this thing has."

"Sure."

As he climbed up, Tyler gave me a thumbs-up.

We pulled into the marina and tied up. Tyler and Atlas got off. We handed off their gear, and Atlas said, "I still can't believe we didn't win this. The bastards rigged it."

I said, "We came in second, that's not bad."

"It sucks, we should've won first prize."

"We'll get them next time."

"Anytime you want to go out, let me know."

"I'd love to, you tell me when."

"How about Friday?"

"Sounds good."

"Laura! You want to go fishing Friday? Atlas is coming out with me."

"Yeah, that'll be fun."

His lottery-winner smile said it all.

Mario eased the throttle forward and we pulled away from the dock as I raised the bumpers.

I waved Laura over and we congregated around Mario, who asked, "Did the kid do what he had to?"

"Yes. It went smooth as silk. His father had no idea."

Laura said, "What a jerk."

Mario chimed in, "I still can't believe he stuffed that fish with sinkers."

I said, "It's actually a pretty good way to cheat."

Laura said, "He's a sleazebag. He was practically drooling over me."

"You played it perfectly. Thanks."

"It was fun helping you."

"You're up for another role on Friday, and this one is a biggie."

"What?"

"I'll tell you later."

Sitting at one of the outdoor tables Seventh South Waterfront had, I nursed a Tito's on the rocks and waited for Mario. He arrived more than twenty minutes late, pulling into a spot in the parking lot.

"Sorry, man. Got kinda hung up with Susan." He smiled.

"I'm not looking for details."

"How do you and Laura get along, you know, sex-wise?"

"I don't talk about stuff like that. You want something?"

He picked up the drink menu. "I'm going to get one of these IPAs."

A server came over and Mario said, "I love the name: I'll try a Riptide Porpoise Party."

I shook my head as the waiter left. "That's a wild name for a beer."

I winced moving my leg. "It's good marketing."

"How's the leg?"

"Not too bad. Did you get anything more on our Russian friend?"

Mario waited until the server put his drink down. He took a sip and wiped his lips with the back of his hand. "This is good. You want to try?"

"No. What about Igor?"

"You were right, there's a connection to the Bratva, the Russian mob out of New York. They operate a human smuggling ring to the States. They get East Europeans onto ships and run them into Cuba and other Caribbean islands, and from there get them to South Florida."

"That lines up with the info Larson got. They charge astronomical fees to get out of places like Moldova and Belarus, and when they can't pay it, they have to work it off by becoming prostitutes."

"And when they get hooked on drugs, which they supply for nothing, they're never able to repay it."

"How close are the ties between Igor and them?"

"It looks like he just buys some of his girls from them. He operates mainly out of Orlando but has places in Tampa and Fort Myers."

"How many women?"

"Estimates are around a hundred."

"Jesus. What about the trouble you mentioned with his people?"

"There's rumors of a possible split."

"I don't know if that is good or bad for Bev."

"Do you really think Bev is trapped up there?"

I shook my head. "I hope like hell she isn't, but we have nothing else to go on. It's like she dropped off the face of the earth."

"Well, being in something like this shit Igor has going is the perfect place. She'd be isolated and—"

"I know. Believe me, I know. It's what scares me, and it fits with her not having a driver's license or anything that leaves a trace."

"I hope she's okay."

"We can't wait. We have to make a move."

"What are you thinking? Should we go up there and confront Igor?"

"We have to, but we have to do something with the Atlas Crane case first."

"What can I do to help?"

I leaned in. "You're going to play a small but critical role."

He smiled. "I like it already. Tell me about it."

21

———

I PULLED UP TO MAGNOLIA SQUARE AND WAITED IN THE SHADE for Laura to come down. She smiled and put her sunglasses on before hopping into my Beemer.

She pecked my cheek. "How's your leg?"

"It's good. It hasn't bled in a while."

"That's good. Keep it clean and change the dressing every day."

"I am. So, are you ready?"

She nodded. "Oh yeah. This is so exciting. I can see why you like what you do."

Turning onto Livingston Road, I said, "Don't get used to it. I don't want you involved in this stuff."

"Why not?"

"Because it can go wrong real fast."

"Oh, come on—"

"Laura, this isn't the movies, this is dangerous stuff we're doing."

"We're just going to embarrass Atlas, make him look like the jerk he is. Frankly, he deserves it."

"It's way more than yanking somebody around."

"What do you mean?"

"You'll see, but right now we have to play this perfectly."

"Don't worry. I got this."

"Let's go over it again."

"I told you, I know what to do."

"Well, let's review it one more time for me before we get to Atlas's house."

Atlas was in his garage when we pulled up. He waved and picked up his fishing rod. I stepped out of the car. "You don't need to bring any gear. I bought the rods you said were the best. They're on the boat ready to use."

"Really?"

"Yes. I didn't want to be bothered carrying stuff back and forth all the time."

He set his rod down. "It must be nice to have money."

"You can't take it with you."

Getting in the car, I moaned, "Ouch!"

Atlas said, "Your leg?"

"Yeah, it's acting up today. Hop in."

Atlas got in the back seat. "Hey, Laura, how's it going?"

She batted her eyes. "Better since you got in."

He smiled. "What's the matter, is Beck giving you a hard time?"

"Nah, it's just nice to see you."

"Same here. We're going to have great day."

"Definitely. It's so beautiful out."

I turned onto Livingston Road and Laura's phone rang.

"Hello?"

"Oh hi, how are you?"

"I'm with Beck and his handsome friend. We're going on Beck's boat. Why?"

She put her hand up. "That's no problem. We're like, five minutes from there.

No problem. We'll drop her off at your mother's. Don't worry, feel better."

She hung up, and I said, "What's going on?"

"Make a U-turn. Melissa is running late and needs someone to pick up Diane. She goes to the Community School by Orange Blossom Drive."

"Sure thing."

Laura turned her head. "You don't mind, do you?"

Atlas said, "Of course not. Your friend needs help."

"Thanks. Her mother lives in Kensington, just a mile or two away."

"No worries."

Pulling into the school's parking lot, Laura said, "Oh boy, all of a sudden, my stomach is doing flips."

I said, "What's the matter?"

"I don't know, I think I'm going to throw up or something."

Atlas said, "Open your window, get some air."

She rolled down her window and pointed, "There's Diane."

I said, "I'll go get her."

Laura said, "No. You said your leg was hurting."

"It's not that bad."

Laura faked a burp. "Atlas, can you get Diane for me?"

"Sure. Which one is she?"

"Diane's the one with the blonde hair, with the blue top on, standing to the left. Her mother is Melissa."

"No problem." He opened the car door. "I'll be right back."

I opened my window, and the heat rushed in. I watched Atlas follow a couple of parents toward the pickup area.

He approached the girl Laura identified and started talking

to her. The kid backed up and Atlas took a step toward her, reaching for her hand. The kid screamed, and a man stepped in between her and Atlas.

Two other adults rushed over. Atlas threw his hands up, pointing at our car. I pocketed my phone and waved.

Laura said, "Did you get that on video?"

"Yes."

"What are you going to do with it?"

I rolled my window up. "We'll talk later."

Atlas pulled open the back door. "What the fuck was that? Was that the right kid?"

"I thought so, she looked like her, but Melissa just sent a text that her mother picked her up. I'm sorry I missed it."

Atlas said, "No worries. How is your stomach feeling?"

"A little bit better, but I don't think going on a boat right now is a good idea."

I said, "That's okay. We'll drop you off, and Atlas and I will go out for a while."

———

After letting Laura out in a different apartment complex from the one she lived in, I said, "Are you ready to go fishing?"

"Absolutely, man. Let's do it."

"I have to make one more stop. If that's okay with you?"

"Sure, man."

Driving east, I moaned, "My frigging leg is acting up."

"You still going to be able to go fishing?"

Turning into a mobile home development, I said, "I hope so. I really have to rest it."

I stopped across the street from a blue trailer with a screenless front door. Stretching for the glove box, I groaned, "Can you get the envelope out?"

Atlas opened the compartment.

Squirming in my seat, I said, "Can you do me a favor and hand this off for me?"

"Sure, no problem."

"Great, just give it to the guy who answers the door."

Atlas got out, and I started filming with my phone. He knocked on the door and a minute later Plas Berry answered the door. Atlas gave him the package and pointed at me before walking back to the car.

"The guy wanted to know what it was."

"It's something a lawyer friend wanted me to drop off, some kind of service process or something to do with a lawsuit."

"A lawsuit?"

"I don't really know, I'm just doing a friend a favor. Let's get on the water."

22

Tyler Crane was sitting at a table outside of the Kilwins in Mercato. Maybe it was the ice cream cone he was licking, but despite being twenty-four, Tyler was a kid in my eyes. Like me, he'd tragically lost his mother. But that was where the similarity ended. To survive, I had to become street-smart, but Tyler was greener than a Granny Smith apple.

"Hey, Tyler."

"Oh, hi, Beck."

"Let's take a walk."

He took a last lick of his cone and dumped the rest in the trash.

We weaved through an endless stream of tourists toward the Tap 42 restaurant.

Tyler said, "My father said he was out on your boat again."

"That's right. It's all part of the plan."

"So, when's it going to happen?"

"Are you still sure you want to go through with it?"

"Yes, why are you asking?"

"It's going to get rough from here."

"As long as he goes to jail for killing Mom, I'm good with whatever happens."

"Did you park where I told you to?"

"Yes."

"Let's cross over."

We silently passed along the side of Rocco's Tacos.

Near the entrance to the parking garage, I asked, "Where's your car?"

He pointed to a silver Honda Civic. We got in, and he reached behind the driver's seat, grabbing a laptop off the back seat.

Tyler tapped in the passcode. "Here you go."

I took it from him. "You're sure about going ahead with this?"

"Yeah, but now you're scaring me."

"This is your last chance to back out."

"No. He's got to pay for killing Mom."

I dug a thumb drive out of my pocket.

"What's that?"

"You don't need to know."

I uploaded the contents onto his father's laptop.

Handing the laptop back, I said, "Don't bother trying to look at it, it's encrypted, using a military protocol."

"Military protocol? What the heck is that?"

"Get this back in the house straightaway. He can't know it's been missing."

"I will."

"I mean it. Go right to his place and put the laptop back. Make sure it's exactly where you found it."

"Okay."

I pulled out a burner phone and gave him the number. "Now, I'd like you to text me a picture of your mother."

"What kind of picture?"

"It doesn't matter, but a picture around the time she was murdered would be good."

He scrolled through his phone. "This is a good one. It was a real photo, and I took a picture of it with my phone. I remember the day, she was in a really good mood."

"Send it."

"What are you going to do with it?"

"Just send it."

The burner vibrated. I opened the text and looked at the picture of his mother.

"Okay. I've got to leave. Go straight to your father's place."

I walked to the Whole Foods parking lot and got in my car. Opening the burner phone, I attached the photo of Ana Crane to a text.

Before sending it, I added a message: *Atlas, we know you killed her. It's time to confess.* About to turn onto Route 41, the burner pinged. It was a text reply from Atlas: *Who the fuck is this?*

Tossing the phone on the passenger seat, I smiled.

Acknowledging Sugar Shack had invigorated downtown Bonita Springs, I found a parking spot two blocks away. A rock band that leaned country was on stage. I took a table as far away as possible and ordered a Tito's on the rocks.

Before my drink came, Detective Moreno pulled out a chair. "Boy, the music is loud as hell here."

I flagged a server. "That it is."

Moreno ordered a beer and said, "So, what's so delicate you couldn't tell me on the phone."

"I wanted to show you something."

"What do you have?"

I put up a hand and waited until our drinks were set down.

Moreno raised his glass. I clinked it and took a sip of my vodka.

Scooting my chair close, I palmed my phone. "Take a look at these."

I played the video of Atlas Crane at the Naples Community School I'd taken.

"What's going on?"

"It might have been an attempted kidnapping of a child."

Moreno scrunched his nose. "In broad daylight, with witnesses?"

"He apparently told the others he was picking her up for the girl's mother."

"Who is this guy?"

"That's the thing. You remember the murder of Ana Crane in Livingston Estates years ago?"

"The one where the husband was charged?"

"Yes. This guy is the husband, Atlas Crane. He got off when a key witness died in a car accident before he could testify."

He nodded. "Right, I remember now."

"I think you should alert the Sex Crimes Unit."

"If this is all you got, they'd laugh at me."

"No, I have more. Check this out."

I played the video of Atlas Crane delivering the envelope to the man in the trailer.

"Okay. What am I looking at?"

"That's Atlas Crane again, and the man he's passing the manila envelope to is John Hack."

"And what makes this so important?"

"John Hack is a convicted sex offender. He was trafficking in child pornography."

Moreno shook his head. "Bastards."

"I'm told Atlas Crane is mixed up in distributing child porn. It's something you need to look into."

"You know we'd need proof to make a move, and these videos are circumstantial at best."

"I've also been tipped off Crane has a storage unit, one that he rented under an alias, at CubeSmart Self Storage. He's probably keeps a stash of that crap there."

"Who told you that?"

"I can't say more than that the source is a trusted one. Someone who has been right every time."

"It'll be tough to get a warrant to search a unit with what you have."

"Take a look at this."

I played him a video of the sex offender John Hack and another man at CubeSmart Self Storage.

"That's the same man at the trailer. Who is the other man?"

"Steve Weintraub. He's another convicted sex offender. Served six years for possession of child porn."

He winced. "What the hell do these sickos get out of crap like this?"

"They're mentally ill. You can't fix people like them."

"You know, I could never work in the Sex Crimes Unit. It's more upsetting than working homicide."

"Tough on your stomach and mind."

"You're confident Crane is using this unit for porn?"

Pulling out two documents from my pocket, I said, "See you for yourself. He used a driver's license with his picture but under a different name to rent the unit. Why would you do that if you weren't hiding something?"

Moreno examined the documents. "This is a high-quality forgery."

The detective was right, but then again, Igor's operation produced impeccable counterfeits. "Can you convince the sex unit to do a raid, see what's in that unit? It'd be great to get these mutts off the street."

"We've gotten warrants approved when a confidential informant has a track record. Give me the source and I'll see where it goes. If they could get it in front of Judge Kennedy, he'd sign a warrant."

"I can't reveal the source. Besides, you don't need the name of the informant for the judge."

"True, but it's my neck on the line with the sex unit guys."

"I trust this informant. It won't be a bust, I promise."

"I don't know."

"Come on, Mo. Have I ever steered you wrong?"

23

A PAIR OF BLACK SUVs TURNED OFF AIRPORT PULLING ROAD and barreled down World Trade Center Way. Detective Moreno, a passenger in the lead car, said, "It's right by Smith and DeShields."

Robert Ryan, who was running the operation, pointed at a red-roofed building, "Okay, here we go."

He pulled into the driveway for CubeSmart Self Storage and came to a stop by the office for the business.

He said, "Moreno, it's unit 47A, right?"

"Yes. Looks like it's to the right."

Ryan went into the office for a minute. He came out when the gate opened.

The lead agent steered between two buildings. Each cinder block structure contained a dozen red garage doors. He slowed and stopped in front of the next-to-last unit. "This is it."

Two men got out of each of the vehicles. They all put on gloves. An agent with bolt cutters snapped the padlock off. A gloved hand yanked the door's handle, and the garage door rolled up.

The steel interior walls of the golf-cart-sized space were

lined with cardboard boxes. Ryan pointed to a filing cabinet. "Moreno, why don't you go through that?"

"I got it."

"You two, get to work on the boxes."

As the officers stepped inside, Ryan turned around. "We've got company."

A white van plastered with the WINK News logo pulled up.

Ryan said, "Who the hell leaked this?"

As Moreno wrestled with the lock on the filing cabinet, Ryan went toward a woman getting out of the van. "Stay in your vehicle!"

"We're just here observing. Can you tell us what you're looking for?"

"All I can say is we're executing a search warrant."

The cameraman accompanying her boosted his video camera onto a shoulder, aiming it at the unit in question.

The reporter asked, "Who does the unit belong to?"

"I'm not going to comment further."

"We'll get the information, Officer."

"Stay back or I'll have you arrested for obstruction."

"Can't you share a little something on this?"

"Stand back and stay put. Don't test me. You get an inch closer, I'll slap cuffs on both of you."

Moreno popped the lock out and opened the top drawer. It was empty. He slammed it shut and pulled the next drawer out.

"I think we got something."

Moreno snapped pictures as Ryan came over.

The lead agent asked, "Are those hard drives?"

"Yep. You see the labels?"

They all read Confidential.

Moreno picked one up and turned it over. "What's this mean?"

It had a sticker of a peach on it.

Ryan said, "That's pedo code for a kid's bottom."

"Jesus." Moreno took a second one out, flipping it over.

"Even I know what jalapeno means."

"Bag the drives."

Moreno slipped them into evidence bags and opened the last drawer. A manila envelope labeled Special Collection stared at him. He snapped a picture and turned it over. His stomach turned when he saw what was written in magic marker: Under Six Years Old.

He picked up the envelope, lifted the flap, and looked inside. It was empty. He put it in a bag and closed the drawer.

Ryan was kneeling next to a toolbox. He took a Polaroid picture out of it as another officer said, "We got a cell phone."

Ryan shook his head and said, "I'm going to call for another unit."

Two hours later, an officer pulled the garage door down and sealed it with crime scene tape. The woman reporter shouted questions as the raid team got into their vehicles.

Back at the Collier County Sheriff's Office, they grabbed coffee and sat around a conference table.

Ryan picked up a clipboard. "Let's go over what we have and figure out our next move."

"We've got five boxes of new toys and stuffed animals."

"This snake is using them to lure kids."

"Probably, but that's a shitload of toys. How many kids is this bastard going after?"

"What about the cell phone?"

"It's a burner with only one contact: Willie Wonka."

"This is one sick motherfucker. I'd like to—"

"Forensics is going over it in more detail, but they found a draft of a text that was never sent. It was asking for a new shipment."

"Is this guy supplying or looking to buy porn?"

"Unknown at this point, but the maps highlighting schools and playgrounds is concerning as hell. As are the pictures of kids."

"The ones taken at Venetian Village were shot with a high-powered lens. Maybe this shithead lives around there."

Moreno said, "We have enough to bring him in."

24

USING THE REMOTE, I ADJUSTED THE TV'S VOLUME AND WENT into the kitchen.

Laura was washing spinach leaves in the sink and said, "What's wrong with you? The TV is crazy loud."

"I want to watch something on the news."

I peeked at the TV. Sitting behind a console, a newscaster said, "We'll look at the weather for the weekend right after we bring you this developing story. Let's go to Katherine Rigby."

I rushed to the family room and sat in front of the TV as the screen filled with an image of a female reporter. "Thank you, Bill. I'm standing outside the CubeSmart Self Storage facility on World Trade Center Way.

"The Collier County Sex Crimes Unit conducted a search of a particular container."

Video footage of officers carrying cartons and bags of evidence replaced the reporter, who said, "Agents emptied the storage unit, putting the contents into their vans.

"We asked who we believe to be the lead agent for a comment, but they refused to talk to us. WINK News has been able to identify the person who rented the unit from CubeSmart Self Storage, a Mr. Morris Fry.

"WINK News is trying to contact Mr. Fry but has been unable to reach him. We'll update you on the nature of the seizure as we learn more."

As the newscaster said, "It looks like we've got a picture-perfect weekend coming up. We'll look at the weather right after this commercial break," Laura came into the room. "Is that storage thing something you're involved in?"

"No."

"Then why are you watching it?"

She was hard to fool, but I was quick. "Detective Moreno said he was going to be on TV."

"Oh. Did you see him?"

I clicked off the news. "Yeah, he was carrying something they seized from a storage unit."

"You're meeting him later, right?"

"He wants to meet for a quick drink."

"Why?"

She'd make a good interrogator, but I was born cagey. "I don't know, maybe he wants to revel in his TV appearance."

"But you just saw him the other night."

"Yeah, but maybe he's got some information on Bev. He's the one who tracked her to Orlando."

"Do you think you'll find her?"

Shrugging, I said, "I hope so. I have to check on Dawn. It's been a week since I had time to stop over there."

She pinched her face.

I said, "What?"

"You kind of made her my responsibility."

"No, no, no. That's not true. I appreciate everything you're doing for her, but I'm the one who started all this."

"All this?"

"You know, me finding her and making sure she and Abby weren't going to be homeless again. I don't care if I have to pay for it."

"You do realize it's not all about the money. Dawn needs a roof over her head and food in the fridge, but what's more important is that she needs someone she can trust, somebody to guide her. Her mother left her, and while her finding a way to survive is amazing, to thrive, she's going to need the tools to make a decent living, be a good mother, and socially interact with the rest of the world."

I stared at Laura. She sounded like a social worker. "I know it's not just money. She needs a support system, and if we can find Bev, it can't hurt."

"Are you sure about that? From what I've learned from you, Bev has her own set of issues to deal with."

"I'm sure she does, but I can't let her stay stuck in the life she's in now."

"I understand, but as nice as it sounds, reuniting Bev with Dawn may not be good for Dawn and Abby."

I threw up my hands. "What am I supposed to do? Forget about Bev? I can't do that again."

"I'm not saying to forget about her, I'm just trying to make sure you understand how complicated this is. You need—"

"I can't talk about this now, I've got to meet Moreno."

Streaks of red ran across the sky as a sliver of the sun capped the horizon. Perched on a chair at the far end of Gumbo Limbo, I nursed my vodka and waited for Detective Moreno.

Moreno waved as he strode over. He was wearing shorts and a Tommy Bahama shirt. We shook and he ordered a beer.

He said, "It's been a while since I've been here. This view is the best in town."

"It is, but in season, it's too crowded. Waiting an hour for a table isn't something I'll ever do."

"Most of the people waiting are staying here, so I guess it's not a big deal for them."

"And the Ritz gets to sell them twenty-dollar drinks as they wait."

He asked, "Is that how much they charge?"

"Don't worry, I got it."

The server brought Moreno's beer and left.

Softening my voice, I said, "So, tell me about the raid."

Moreno took a sip and said, "It looks like the information you gave is first-rate."

I smiled. "Did you expect any less?"

He scoffed. "We found a bunch of what appears to be incriminating evidence, including a couple of hard drives."

"What was on them?"

"We don't know. They're encrypted with military-grade security. We may have to ask the FBI for help."

"Wow. That's suspicious. Anything else?"

"We found a slew of pictures of kids and maps where schools and playgrounds were highlighted."

"Jesus, this guy is a serious pedophile."

Moreno nodded. "He had boxes and boxes of toys and stickers that the sex unit said were code in the child porn world."

I exhaled. "This crap makes me sick."

"I'm with you."

"Anything else interesting?"

"A burner phone but only one contact. And get this, the contact was Willie Wonka."

"Did you do a search to see if anyone is using that alias?"

"Come on, of course we did, but we got nothing."

"I didn't mean it that way."

He nodded. "We're going over the phone to see if they can retrieve anything that was deleted."

"This guy might have gotten away with murdering his wife, but you're going to nail him now."

"Did you mention the raid to anybody?"

"Me? Who would I tell?"

"Did you say anything to Mario? Larson?"

"No. I kept it to myself. Why?"

"Minutes after we pulled up to the storage facility, a WINK News van showed up."

My eyes widened. "They did?"

"Yeah, I thought you might have said something to Mario, and he told someone."

"I never said a word, and he wouldn't do that anyway."

Moreno nodded. "I guess there's a leak in the sex unit because I never even told the sheriff the particulars of what I was working on."

"The important thing is Crane wasn't tipped off."

"For sure. If we came up empty, it would've been a disaster for me."

"Are you going to bring Atlas Crane in?"

"Yes. They're just waiting to see if they can pull anything off the drives and the phone before making a move."

25

I hopped back in my car and checked the time: 8:45 p.m. Was it too late to stop by Dawn's apartment? She probably had put Abby to bed by now, but if I went there, I might wake the baby up.

Forget it. I'd try to go tomorrow.

I started the car and opened the glove box. I took the new burner phone out of its packaging.

After activating it, I typed out a message to Atlas Crane: *Confess to murdering your wife, Ana, or you're going to regret it. Believe me, it's going to get much worse for you.*

I hit send and pulled away from the curb.

Before I got to the next light, the burner phone pinged. I smiled and slowed to catch the next red signal.

Atlas Crane had replied: *Fuck off! You asshole!*

I tapped out a reply: *This is no game. Confess to killing your ex-wife while you still have time.*

What are you talking about? I'm innocent.

We both know you're guilty as sin.

Fuck you!

Are you going to confess?

I said fuck you!

The car behind me honked its horn as I hit send on my last reply: *You leave me no choice.*

I hit the gas and drove on Route 41 for a couple of miles before pulling into a Walmart's parking lot. Coming to a stop in a far corner, I dialed a number and held a voice modulator in front of my mouth.

The WINK News reporter answered, "Hello?"

"Do you trust me now?"

"Who is this?"

"The person who tipped you off on the CubeSmart Storage raid."

"Oh. Thank you. Do you have something more?"

"The unit belongs to Atlas Crane. He rented it using a fake ID."

"Atlas Crane? Are you sure?"

"A thousand percent."

"How do you know this?"

I cut the call off and put the burner and voice changer in the glove box. Using my regular cell phone, I punched in another number.

Atlas Crane answered on the first ring. "Beck?"

"Hey, Atlas, I know it's late, but I just decided to go fishing tomorrow, and I wanted to see if you wanted to go."

He hesitated. "Um, I don't know."

"What's the matter? You sound stressed or something."

"It's nothing. Forget about it."

It was easy to picture the scowl on his face.

"You can tell me, man. Maybe I can help."

There was a long pause before Atlas said, "I've been getting these crazy calls, well, they're texts. But that's all."

"What do you mean? From who?"

"I don't know."

"What are they saying?"

"All kinds of bullshit, that I killed my wife, and I should confess or they're going to do something."

"Confess to killing your wife? That's crazy."

"I know. I told them to screw off but . . ."

"Forget about them, it sounds like a nutjob with an axe to grind."

"You're probably right, but the whole thing feels weird, you know?"

"I get it, this thing's got you jumpy."

"I don't know why, but it does."

"Come on the boat tomorrow, it's just what you need."

"That sounds really good."

"I've got something in the morning. What do say about meeting me around two o'clock. We'll fish for a couple of hours and grab dinner afterward."

"I look forward to it. Thanks."

"No problem. You'll be back to yourself before we hook the first fish."

He laughed and I hung up.

I waited an hour before sending Atlas a text message: *If you don't confess to killing your wife, you're going to be tagged with something worse, much worse. Time is running out.*

His reply came immediately: *Leave me the fuck alone.*

I replied: *We're going to nail you, so you better confess or it's going to be worse for you.*

Get the fuck out of here, what could be worse than admitting to murder? Especially since I didn't do it.

You sure did, and if you don't think it'll be ten times rougher for you, try me.

Please leave me alone.

Atlas had suddenly got manners. I waited until I was about to climb into bed before sending him another message from the burner. The last one of the day was short: *Ticktock.*

I HOPPED OUT OF BED. TOBY FOLLOWED ME TO THE KITCHEN. I put the coffee machine on, grabbed his leash, and a burner phone.

Turning the burner on, I said, "Come on, boy. We're going for a walk."

The sun was peaking over the tree line as Toby squatted. As he did his business, I sent a text message to Atlas: *You don't have much time to stop it. Are you going to confess to the murder?*

Never. I didn't do it.

You're in denial and time is almost up.

You can't fool me with your bullshit.

This is no game, Atlas. I know it's tough to imagine something worse than being a murderer but you're going to regret it.

Using a poop bag, I picked up what Toby left and tied the top of the bag. I gave him a treat, and we headed back to the house.

We were greeted with the smell of coffee. I poured a cup, figuring I had a couple of hours free. Using my regular cell, I called Dawn.

"Good morning, Dawn."

"Hey, how are you doing, Beck? Is everything okay?"

"Yes. Everything is good. I wanted to stop over, are you going to be around?"

"When?"

"In a little while."

"Uh, okay. I guess."

I was there in under thirty minutes. Dawn was still in her pajamas, and the place smelled like french fries.

After a quick hug, I surveyed the room.

"I have to clean up. I was going to, but Abby acted up . . ."

The place resembled a pigsty. Clothes were all over the place, and the coffee table was crowded with dirty plates and an empty pizza box.

"You can live anyway you want, but be careful because Abby is going to pick up your habits."

Her eyes flared with anger. "I've been busy."

"How is work going?"

She shrugged. "They gave me so much work, it's stressing me out."

"I was thinking it might be a good idea to go to school for something in the medical field."

"Medical?"

"You know, like an X-ray technician or somebody who does ultrasounds."

"I don't really like school, and besides, I've got to take care of Abby."

"We can figure out what to do with Abby. Before you know it, she'll be going to school, and you'll have plenty of free time."

"When the time comes, I'll see about doing something different."

I was tempted to ask if that included doing the laundry that was piled up by the bathroom. "You can't wait till then. You have to prepare in advance if you want to succeed. You start now and you'll be ready when the time comes."

"I'm okay the way things are."

"Look, and don't take this the wrong way, but this apartment, the food and everything, you couldn't afford it on what you make."

"Don't throw it in my face, okay? I didn't ask you for help."

"I know that. I'm happy to help you guys. I'm just trying to make sure you and Abby have a good life."

"We're doing good."

My phone pinged with a text. Detective Moreno wanted to know if I was free to talk.

I replied and said to Dawn, "I've got to run. I think Laura is going to stop by later."

"Okay."

"Think about what I said about learning a technical skill so you can make a decent living."

She rolled her eyes. I said goodbye and headed outside wondering if this was the type of stuff parents had to deal with.

I sidestepped a sprinkler, jumped in my BMW, and called Moreno.

"Hey, Mo, what's up?"

"Since you're the one who tipped us off to Crane in the first place, I wanted to tell you we're bringing him in."

"Good. Does he know?"

"Not yet. We're watching his house and are going to send a car to his place at noon."

"What about a search warrant? Aren't you worried he'll destroy evidence?"

"They felt we didn't have enough to get a warrant."

"Didn't you get anything from forensics?"

"Nothing yet."

"What do you mean? What about the hard drives?"

"Even the Feds couldn't decipher the encryption. They're still working on it, but we're not counting on it."

"He must have some crazy stuff on it to go that far to keep it hidden."

"That's what we believe and why we want to talk to him. Maybe he'll crack."

"I don't know. If this guy held it together during a murder trial, he's probably not going to give you much."

"We'll find out this afternoon."

"I wish I could be a fly on the wall."

I finished the call and made another one. Assured that a critical piece of my plan was going to happen, I sped home.

27

___

Toby was waiting by the interior garage door. He put his paws on my thighs, and I rubbed his head.

"Come on, boy. Do you want to go for a ride?"

Toby barked as I clipped his leash on.

"How about we go to the park?"

I drove to North Collier Regional Park and, holding my cell phone, I took Toby on a walk. Circling back from the soccer fields, a text came in. They were minutes away.

"Let's go, boy."

Toby led the way back to the car. The timing seemed perfect. I headed south on Livingston and turned onto the street Atlas Crane lived on.

A WINK News van was sitting in front of his house. As I pulled behind it, a reporter and her cameraman were at the front door talking to Atlas.

Crane stepped outside shaking his head. I opened the car door and could hear him say, "No way. There's been some kind of mistake."

"Then why did the police raid the self-storage unit you rented?"

"I don't have a storage unit."

"Come on, Mr. Crane, you rented it under an alias."

"This is crazy. I don't know what the heck is going on. It's a mistake, you got to believe me. Here, here's my friend, he knows the kind of person I am."

I put a ball cap on and, holding a hand in front of my face, I walked up with Toby saying, "I don't want to be on camera—and Atlas, it's not a good idea to talk to the press. Tell them you want them off your property."

Atlas nodded. "Yeah, get off my property! Now, before I call the cops."

The reporter motioned to the cameraman, and they walked toward the street.

I said, "What do they want?"

"It's some kind of mix-up."

"What did they say?"

He signaled to a pair of neighbors who were gathered across the street. "It's a mistake. Go home."

He turned to me. "Come in. We'll talk inside."

"I can't stay. I was at the park with Toby and figured I'd stop by to tell you I can go fishing earlier than two. You still going?"

"Holy shit!"

"What?"

"Remember I told you somebody was threatening me?"

"Yes, why?"

"I think that's why they're here."

"I don't understand."

He looked across the street where a group of neighbors were talking to the reporter.

"Let's go inside."

We stepped into the foyer. I said, "Why is WINK news here in the first place?"

"They think I'm some kind of pervert."

"What? Why would they think that?"

"I don't know. They said something about some stuff the police found in a storage unit, but I don't even have one."

"Are you sure?"

"Of course I'm sure. This is some kind of big screwup."

"You said something about some guy calling or texting you. What's that all about?"

"Nothing, just some angry bitch telling me to confess to Ana's murder or something worse is going to happen to me."

"Worse than admitting to killing someone?"

His cell rang and he dug it out of his pocket, saying, "I know, it's crazy, right?"

I said, "Get that. I'm betting it's the people who've been hassling you."

"Hello?"

"Yeah, that's me."

"What? Why?"

The color drained from his face. "What questions?"

"When?"

"What if I don't want to go?"

"Okay, okay. I'll go."

He disconnected the call. I said, "Is everything all right?"

Atlas hung his head.

I asked, "Who was that?"

"The police. They're sending a car to take me in."

"Why?"

"They said they have questions to ask me."

"About what?"

"They didn't say. I bet you it's gonna be about Ana, which is bullshit. That was settled a long time ago."

"Do you think they might have gotten new evidence or something?"

"I don't care what they got. They can't do shit because of double jeopardy."

"Double jeopardy? What's that?"

"Nobody can be tried again if they were found not guilty, like me."

"That's great. So, what are you worried about?"

He shrugged. "I guess you're right."

"Just go and see what they want. If it gets crazy, hire a lawyer and sue them for harassment."

He smiled. "That's a good idea."

"Let me know how you make out. I'll check my calendar to see about us going fishing another day. Maybe I'll ask Laura to come."

"Yeah, that'd be sweet."

I tugged my cap lower, opened the door, and stepped outside. Shielding my face, I saw a dozen of his neighbors gathered around the reporter. Most turned, looking our way. A man pointed down the block.

A patrol car rolled up the street and stopped in front of Atlas's house.

I hopped in my car as a uniformed officer got out of his. I rolled down my window as he went up to the door. Atlas opened it and the officer said something to him. Atlas disappeared into the house.

A minute later, Atlas came out and followed the cop to the patrol car. As he got into the rear of the car, one of the neighbors shouted, "Lock the predator up and throw away the key."

Another yelled, "Castrate the bastard!"

I drove a block away and pulled over. Using the burner phone, I sent a text message to Atlas: *Confess to your wife's murder or you're going to be sorry.*

28

———

My singing along with Steely Dan's "Peg" was interrupted by the doorbell. I left Laura in the kitchen and peeked out the window; it was Mario. I opened the door.

My foster brother said, "It smells good in here. What are you making?"

"My famous pork chops. You want to stay for dinner?"

"Nah, I can't. Susan and me are going to the movies with her parents."

Laura said, "Well, that's nice. How often do you see her mother and father?"

"Every couple of weeks. They're cool. Her old man is a really good bowler."

"Let me ask you, when you guys moved in together, was it a big change?"

"I don't know, it just kind of happened, you know what I mean?"

I knew I'd be catching an attitude from Laura and said, "I need to talk to Mario. The water is boiling, can you throw the pasta in?"

A flash of anger crossed her face, but she said, "Sure."

I tapped Mario's arm. "Let's go onto the lanai."

Closing the sliding door behind us, I asked, "How did you make out in Orlando?"

"Check this out."

He handed me a picture.

"Holy shit. It's Bev."

"Where'd you get it?"

"I paid a grand to one of the Albanians."

"I'll pay you back." I fingered the picture. "I can't believe it. You see the jacket?"

"Yeah."

"She always wanted to be a ballerina. This is great. It means she's alive."

"Yeah."

"What's the matter?"

"We got a problem."

"What?"

"You know the fake driver's license for Atlas Crane we rented the storage unit with?"

"Yes, what about it?"

"Guess who runs that operation?"

"That's Blinkie's."

Mario shook his head. "Nope, he told me he reports to Igor."

"Igor, the Russian?"

"Yep, and he's pissed."

"Screw him. Does he have Bev?"

"Probably. But he's threatening to tell the cops it was bogus if we push him."

"That would be crazy."

"Yeah, but Igor is a crazy motherfucker. Remember that shit he pulled in Fort Myers?"

"So, he's got Bev, and if we press him, he wants to rat on us?"

"That's what Blinkie told me."

"Why the hell would he do that?"

"He's crazy."

"Did you find out where she is?"

"No, I asked a million times, but he wouldn't say. He said Igor would cut his tongue out before killing him."

"What about the Albanians? Did you get anything?"

"It looks like they did sell her to Igor."

I shook my head. "Sold her? You got confirmation?"

"Not for her exactly, but two people told me that's what they do. They push addicts into prostitution, use them, and sell them off before they fall apart."

"We need to find Bev, and fast."

"What do you want to do?"

Laura opened the slider. "The pasta is done. I'm hungry, how much longer are you going to be?"

"We're coming in now."

As she turned around, I softened my voice and told Mario, "We can't have Igor blowing up the Crane case. So lay off for the moment. I have to think about this."

"Sure, man."

Laura said, "Are you sure you don't want to stay for dinner?"

"I can't, we're getting together with Susan's parents."

He'd told her that five minutes ago. It was her way of resending the message.

We said goodbye and Mario walked out. I wanted to leave with him but closed the door behind him.

Laura giggled.

I said, "What's so funny?"

"Seeing you squirm."

I opened the door to the fridge and took the plate of pork chops out. "I wasn't squirming."

She scoffed. "You sure were."

I put some olive oil in the skillet on the stove.

"You know I don't really care what anybody else does. I'm just concerned about us."

I lit the burner. "Concerned?"

"Not concerned, but, you know, I just want us to go forward, like other couples do."

I didn't want to point out she'd contradicted herself on what other people did. "We're moving forward."

"You only met my parents like two times."

So, it was about her family. "Set something up with them if it makes you happy."

"Really?"

I remembered Larson telling me he'd agreed to things to keep the peace and make his wife happy.

"Sure."

"When do you want to do it? Maybe next weekend?"

I slid the pork chops into the sizzling oil. "Check with them and see what their schedule looks like."

"It doesn't matter, they'll drop everything to get together with us."

"Just throw out some dates and we'll pick one."

She picked up her phone. I would bet everything I had she was calling her mother. She stepped onto the lanai, and I finished making dinner.

We began clearing the table. I said, "The chops came out good tonight."

"I liked the spinach puree. Where'd you get that idea from?"

I pointed to my temple. "It's all in here."

She shook her head, and I checked the time. I went into the family room to turn the TV on.

The segment was supposed to air at 7:15 p.m. I made a call that went to voicemail and left a message: 'Hey man, you should've been there today. It was amazing, I caught four monster groupers. Call me back. I have a couple of dates that work for me and Laura, hopefully you can make it."

Dishtowel in hand, Laura said, "Fishing? Who was that?"

"I called Atlas."

"You want me to go fishing again?"

"It's just a line I'm feeding him."

"But you told him to get some dates."

"He's got bigger things to worry about."

"What's going on?"

Pointing to the TV, I said, "Watch this."

"What is it"

"Just watch, okay?"

Dressed in a dark suit and bright blue tie, a newscaster said, "We're bringing you an update on a story WINK brought to you a couple of days ago. Katherine Rigby is live at the Collier County Sheriff's Office."

"Thank you, Brian. Earlier today, Collier County resident Atlas Crane was brought in for questioning. Mr. Crane is still inside the sheriff's office.

"If you recall, earlier this week, I reported on a story from the CubeSmart Self Storage on World Trade Center Way. The sheriff's office conducted a raid of a storage unit there that WINK News discovered was rented under a false name."

As a gust of wind blew her blonde hair in front of her face, she brushed it away, saying, "It is now alleged that the unit was rented by Atlas Crane, the man you see here being escorted into a patrol car."

The screen displayed Atlas being shown into the back seat of a cop car.

"Mr. Atlas Crane has been questioned for several hours now. Viewers may recall that approximately fourteen years ago, Atlas Crane was acquitted of the murder of his ex-wife, Ana Crane.

"While the Sherriff's Office has not made a statement, a source told WINK News the raid was conducted by the Sex Crimes Unit. The sheriff's office has not confirmed or denied the accusation. We'll bring you an update as soon as we have one.

"This is Katherine Rigby, live from the Collier County Sheriff's Office."

The news anchor reappeared. "Thank you, Katherine. We're going live to Davis Boulevard where an auto accident, involving a fatality and several injured passengers, just occurred."

I clicked the remote.

Laura said, "Sex crimes? And you had me flirting with him?"

I smiled. "You heard her, it's not confirmed."

"No. Seriously, what's going on?"

"I told you this was no game. We get paid to even the score."

"Who hired you?"

Rather than tell her I couldn't say, I said, "Larson handled this one. I don't have any idea."

"Come on, Beck. Don't give me that."

My left pants pocket vibrated. It was the one I kept the

burner phones in. Reaching for it, I said, "I honestly don't know."

I stood and looked at the phone. It was Tyler Crane. Did Laura have a sixth sense?

Why was he calling? A bad feeling came over me as I said, "I've got to take this."

29

TOBY FOLLOWED ME TO THE DOOR. I STEPPED ONTO THE PAVER walkway and closed the door, leaving him behind.

I answered the call. "Hey, Tyler. How is it going?"

"Why don't you tell *me*?"

"I'm not sure I understand."

"My friend called me. He said my father was taken in for questioning. It was on the news."

"That's true. What about it?"

"The news said something about the Sex Crimes Unit. What do they have to do with my mother's murder?"

"Look, I saw the broadcast. You know the news, anything to get ratings."

"Is he being questioned about my mom?"

"I don't know."

"He can't be, right? They can't do anything because of double jeopardy."

"That just means he can't be prosecuted again. There's nothing preventing them from questioning him."

"I guess so. I just didn't like the sex reference thing."

"I told you several times this would get ugly."

"Yeah, but, he's not one of those deviants, it's—"

"Don't start panicking on me. We talked this through. I gave you several chances to end it, but you wanted to get back at him, and that's what I'm doing."

"But not like this."

"It's part of the plan. How did you think he'd confess?"

"But I didn't realize something like this could happen. If I did, I wouldn't do it. Can't we change things up?"

"It's too late, things are in motion."

Tyler said, "If I went to the police and told them, they'd—"

"They'd arrest you! Don't be an idiot!"

"Arrest me? Why would—"

"Calm down and listen to me. You're not going to anyone or opening your mouth. Don't forget, you came to me. Trust me, if you go to the cops, you'll be as sorry as you ever were. Do you hear me?"

His reply was barely audible, "Okay."

I disconnected the call. Considering who might be the bigger threat to tell the authorities, Igor or Tyler, my phone vibrated. It was Atlas Crane.

Taking a deep breath, I swiped the call away.

As I went back into the house, I called out, "Come on, Toby. Let's take a walk." I grabbed his leash, and my cell pinged with a notification. Atlas had left a voicemail.

Telling Laura we'd be right back, Toby tugged on the leash, leading the way outside. I waited until we were a house away to listen to Crane's message.

"Beck, you got to call me right away. I just got back from being grilled by the police. Something's going on, and it's bad. Call me fast, as soon as you get this."

He needed to stew for a while. I'd call him in the morning. Digging out my burner phone, I sent him a text message: *I told you to confess. This is your last warning.*

30

———

MY CELL CHATTERED ON THE KITCHEN TABLE. I SWIPED THE call away and picked up my coffee mug.

Laura said, "That's the third call this morning. Aren't you going to answer it?"

"I'll return the call later."

"Who is it?"

"It's work-related."

She frowned. "What's it about?"

"It's Atlas. The vise is tightening."

"What vise?"

"He killed his wife and got off. We were hired to get justice on him."

"We? Does that include me?"

The real answer was sometimes. "You worked this one and were a great help keeping him distracted."

She smiled. "Does that mean I'm going to get a bonus?"

I reached for her thigh. "Sure. You want it now or later?"

She shook her leg free. "I was talking about money."

"I need to get this over the finish line first. There's a couple of, uh, complications that just came up."

"Let me help you."

I got up and put my cup in the sink. "I might take you up on it, but I need to figure out what to do first."

"I can help, so let me know whatever you need."

"This is unrelated, but can you swing by Dawn's? The place is a pigsty, and I'm starting to worry she's, I don't know, lazy?"

"Being sloppy doesn't mean you're lazy."

"I know, but I suggested she go to school to learn a trade, you know, like being an X-ray technician, but she didn't want to go to school."

"She should become a plumber. They make a lot of money, and she can learn on the job."

"A plumber? She's a woman."

She put her hands on her hips and glared at me.

"It's just that, I've never even seen a lady plumber."

"There's a company called Three Sisters in Naples. Everybody who works there is a woman."

"Fine. If Dawn wants to be a plumber, go for it. Just see if you can talk to her about getting a real job. I don't mind helping her with the bills, but she needs to build her self-esteem, and paying your own way is the best way to do it."

"I'll bring it up."

"Thanks. I'll see you later."

I backed out of the garage and drove three blocks away. I pulled to the curb and dialed a number.

"Hey, Atlas. What happened with the police?"

"They had video from the school. Did you set me up or something?"

"What video?"

"The one where we were going fishing and had to pick up that kid because Lauren's friend was sick or something."

"The school on Livingston?"

"Yeah. They were making like I tried to kidnap the frigging kid."

"That's ridiculous."

"Did you take video of that?"

"No. Why would I do that?"

"How did the cops get it?"

"Somebody is always videoing stuff with their phones. Maybe it was another parent."

"Why'd they go to the cops?"

"Everybody is on the lookout. I think it's because of all the true crime stuff on TV."

"Well, it's a bunch of bullshit."

"I'm sure they realize it was an honest mix-up. What else did they say? Anything about your wife's murder?"

"No, but the whole thing is freaking crazy. They tried to say I had rented a storage unit under a fake name."

"What?"

"They showed me a picture of a driver's license with my picture but a different name."

"That's weird, man. Maybe it was some random picture somebody used. But what's the big deal about the storage unit anyway?"

"They said they found stuff that could be related to child pornography."

"Whoa. What kind of things did they find?"

"They never said, just that there were some hard drives and a phone and toys and some other shit."

"What was on the drives?"

"They wouldn't say."

"This is weird. It sounds like they're fishing."

"Something is going on. Remember I told you about the messages I keep getting?"

"Yes, what about them? You don't think it's related, do you?"

"I don't know what to think. But I'm thinking Ana's sister, Pamela, might be behind this. She's a real bitch and never liked me from day one. When I beat the murder rap, she swore, in front of a bunch of people, that she'd get me one day."

"That explains it. She is probably spreading rumors about you to the police."

"I don't know what to do. I think I'm getting a lawyer, like you said."

"That's your call, but they're expensive. It doesn't sound like the cops have anything or they would have said it already."

"I'm thinking of calling that bitch Pam up and calling her out."

"She'll probably deny it, and she might say you threatened her."

"I'd like to choke the bitch. She was always so nasty to me."

"Calm down. I have a feeling this will blow over."

"You think so?"

"Definitely. They can't waste time on something like this. They probably followed up on what your sister-in-law said to cover their asses."

"That makes sense."

"I have to run to the airport. A cousin of mine took a last-minute trip down. His flight is due any minute. He's going to be in town for a couple of days. I'll call you when he leaves and we'll go fishing."

"All right."

I listened to fifteen minutes of The Daily Stoic podcast before sending Atlas a text message from a burner phone: *Tick-tock. Time is running out. Today is your last day to confess.*

Atlas responded immediately: *Screw you!!!!*

Knowing he was the one about to get screwed, I smiled. But the good feeling never lasted, and this time it vanished before I hit the first stop sign when Mario called.

31

———

Mario said, "Hey, where are you?"

"A block from my house. What's going on?"

"Blinkie told me Igor is going to be in Fort Myers tonight."

"What's he doing there?"

"What do you mean? Igor's been expanding there for two years already. He's got two bars, a couple of whorehouses, and there's a rumor he's going to start a counterfeiting operation in Lehigh Acres."

I said, "If we could get intel on the counterfeiting, it'd be great leverage—"

"I heard the Albanians get ten grand for a prostitute."

My stomach knotted up. "Is that what Igor paid for Bev?"

"Probably something like that."

"What are we in, the damn Middle Ages? How can these low-life bastards be selling people?"

"What are you, living with your head up your ass? Human trafficking is huge, Beck."

"Well, it's fucked up, okay?"

"You ain't got to tell me. I was—"

I said, "I'm going to go see Igor."

"You want me to come?"

"No. I don't want to make this bigger than it is. See if you can find out which place of his he'll be at."

I drove along Colonia Boulevard. Once I hit the corner where the El Patio Restaurant was, I turned onto Cleveland Avenue. To the right was Edison Mall. Opposite it were a couple of auto-body shops and the bar I was heading to.

I made a left, passing along an Asian market into a dark corner of the parking lot. A few cars were in front of the Royal Silk Bar and Grill.

A mountain of a man, who could have been a Sumo wrestler, stood outside the door. He eyed me, threw a chin, and pulled open the door. My eyes adjusted to the reddish hue inside the bar.

I surveyed the half empty room. There was nothing silky or royal about the place. A smattering of Spanish looked to be coming from a pair of bored bartenders. The other language I heard sounded Russian.

Igor wasn't in the room. My eyes settled on a door to the right of the bar. I went up to a bartender.

"What are you having?"

"Nothing right now, but I'm looking for Igor."

"Who's looking?"

"Beck."

The barkeeper spoke in Spanish to the other man behind the bar. He nodded and scooted under the countertop, knocking on the door I had spied.

He disappeared and reappeared minutes later. He said something in Spanish to me. I said, "No habla Espanol."

He said, "Igor is not here."

"I know he is."

He said something in Spanish to the other bartender and laughed.

I walked to the door and pulled it open. "Igor! It's Beck. I need to talk to you."

Three goons rushed over, yanking me back into the main room.

"I need to speak to Igor. He and I do business."

"If Igor wants to speak to you—"

Igor stepped into the doorway. "Let him in."

"Thanks."

"Beck, my friend, what can I do for you?"

"I need to talk, privately."

"Come." He stepped into the back room and waved away two men with shaved heads. As his cronies left, he sat behind a wooden desk and motioned to a chair.

Easing into the seat, I said, "We can settle whatever misunderstanding there is."

"No misunderstanding. You want to disrupt my operations, and Igor cannot allow this. Igor cannot be made to look like a fool."

I'd met a couple of people who talked about themselves in the third person. It was called illeism and was a method to express authority or create distance from something they were responsible for.

"We've known each other a long time. You know I would never try to do that. That's why I came here, to talk man to man."

"Igor always liked you. But now, you are hunting my girls?"

"I'm not hunting just anyone. Bev is my foster sister."

He raised his eyebrows. "Sister?"

"Yes. We were separated when she was ten."

"That is a long time ago. She belongs to Igor now."

"She doesn't belong to anyone."

"Igor paid for her."

"I'll pay you back. How much did you pay Dren?"

"Igor pay ten thousand dollars."

"Okay. I'll bring the money tomorrow."

"Igor needs forty thousand."

"Forty thousand? That's four times what you paid."

"Igor has expenses."

"That's taking advantage, but I'll let it slide."

He nodded.

"I'll be back tomorrow with the cash. Make sure Bev is here."

I floated all the way back to my car. I'd see Bev tomorrow night.

Approaching the ramp for 75 South, I called Mario, but it went to voicemail. I told him to call me and dialed Laura's number.

"Beck? Is everything all right?"

"A million times better than all right."

"What happened?"

"I'm going to pick up Bev tomorrow."

"Oh my God. Really?"

"Yes. I made a deal to get her out of the ring she's with."

"Ring? You said she was, uh, using drugs and selling her body."

"That shit ends now."

"How are you going to prevent her from doing drugs?"

"We'll get her help. I'll get her into a program or something."

"You have to keep in mind the recovery rate is only about fifty percent."

"I'll take that."

"Of course, but nothing is guaranteed."

"So, what the hell do you want me to do? Leave her where she is?"

"Of course not. I just want to be sure your eyes are open."

"They're wide open, okay?"

"I'm not the enemy, Beck. I want you to know I'll do everything I can to help her, but you have to be aware it's going to be ugly. Kicking drugs is hard and messy."

"You think I don't know hard and messy? My mother was murdered, and my father drank himself to death. Me? I was shuffled in and out of foster homes getting my ass kicked left—"

"Take it easy, Beck! Stop attacking me. I'm on your side."

"Sorry."

"We'll do what we can for her. But you have to be realistic about this."

The high from getting close to rescuing Bev evaporated like a Florida puddle. "I know it's going to be tough, but Mario did great after we put him in that Fort Myers place."

"This is different. Bev has probably been using for years; it's ingrained in her lifestyle."

"She had no choice. The system failed her like it did me and Mario. We ran away and survived. I should've taken her with us even though she was too young.

"You have to stop blaming yourself. You were only sixteen."

"Sixteen on paper but thirty in life. Everything would have been different if I hadn't been selfish."

"Stop already. You didn't do anything wrong and now—"

"I feel terrible waiting until now to track her down."

"What did you tell me the other day about looking back? The windshield is bigger for a reason."

I didn't want to hear it, but she was right. "I know, but I can't help obsessing over what happened to her."

"You're doing something about it now. It's all you can do. We'll do our best to help her. And don't forget what you're doing for Dawn and Abby. You're giving them the chance to break the cycle. You're a hero."

I scoffed. "Hero my ass."

"Well, I'm proud of you. Not only for what you're doing for Bev, her daughter and granddaughter, but you're helping get justice for a kid whose mother was murdered."

"It pays the bills."

"That's not why you do it."

She was right, again. "Anyway, can we change the subject?"

"Sure. Oh, I went to see Dawn."

"Was the place a pigsty or what?"

"It was a little messy, but you have to go easy on her, nobody taught her how to take care of a household and a baby."

"What did she say about learning a trade or something?"

"She said she'd think about it. Don't push her or she'll go the other way."

"What are you, a head doctor now?"

"No. But you have to understand she probably has self-esteem issues and zero confidence. She has to be scared to go into something like a vocational school."

"Hmmm."

"You don't think so?"

"No. I have to be honest, I never thought about that."

"It's something she's got to overcome. We all do."

"Do you think you can work with her?"

"Of course."

"I'm afraid of what damage has been done to Bev. I mean, the thought of her being bought and sold makes me sick. I want to shoot the bastards who—"

"One thing at a time. Let's get her first."

"You're right."

"Have you given any thought to where she's going to stay?"

"Uh, I figured she'd stay at the house, so we can keep an eye on her."

"I don't know. She might be better off in a place where professionals can help her."

"That's true. Let me make some arrangements. Maybe the place Mario went to will work."

"That's a good idea. I also heard good things about Oasis Recovery. It's in Fort Myers, close to where Mario went."

"I'll check it out."

"Okay. I'm going to stop by my mother's. The two of them are sick with the flu, and I want to be sure they're okay."

"Okay. Don't catch anything."

32

I took the Pine Ridge exit and headed toward the water. It was a pleasure driving at night on what was usually a congested road. The light at the Airport Pulling Road intersection turned red. As I slowed, the phone rang. It was Mario.

"Hey, how did it go with Igor?"

"He wants forty grand for Bev."

"Forty? He paid Dren only—"

"I don't care. I'm giving him what he wants to get her. Plus, it'll keep his mouth shut about the Crane docs."

"I can't believe it. We're going to be reunited with Bev. Man, I wonder what she's gonna do when she see us."

"You think she'll recognize us?"

"Oh yeah. We look the same as we used to."

That wasn't true. "I made arrangements to get her into Oasis Recovery."

"That's cool. I wonder what she's on."

Exhaling, I said, "It's probably something hard."

"If it was heroin, she'd probably be dead by now."

"Not necessarily. But we'll deal with it. Right now, I need you to come to my house."

Twenty minutes later, I let Mario into my home. He said, "I'm coming with you tomorrow to pick up Bev."

"I don't think it's a good idea."

"Why not?"

"First off, Igor is a wack job. I don't want to introduce anything new into this deal. And besides, we don't know how Bev is going to react. She might be scared, or who knows what?"

"But if she sees us both, it'll make her feel good."

"Maybe, but after everything she's been through, maybe she'll think of us as a threat or something."

"A threat? We're saving her."

"I know, but we don't have a clue as to how she's thinking, and then you throw the drug use in the mix."

"Are you sure she's going to agree to go into rehab?"

"I can't believe she wouldn't want to get clean."

"Don't be so sure. As crazy as it seems, she might believe she deserves the situation she's in."

Was everyone a psychologist? "Let's hope not. But if she resists, I'm going to use Dawn and Abby as leverage."

"That's a good idea, man."

"Let's move the table."

We took opposite sides of the cocktail table and moved it off the area rug. We rolled back the carpet about halfway, revealing the safe built into the floor.

"Mario, under the sink there's a bunch of Publix bags. Grab a couple and double-bag them."

Using my fingerprints and a code, I generated a soft click followed by a blue light. I opened the door and reached inside the safe.

After handing bundles of hundred-dollar bills to Mario, I locked the safe. Mario handed me the bag of money, and I put it under the sink.

We rolled the rug back into place and put the cocktail table back.

I patted Mario on the back. "This time tomorrow, we'll all be together again."

"It's gonna be epic."

"It sure is. We might be a little battered, but we made it, bro. I just hope it's not too late to save Bev."

"I think you should let me come with you to pick her up."

"I got it handled. We need to keep this as low profile as possible for Bev."

"She might try to run."

"Why would she do that? I'm trying to help her."

"She doesn't trust anybody."

"She trusted me more than anybody. Remember how she'd run to me to protect her from that animal, Bryant?"

"I still can't figure out why someone like Bryant got approved to foster kids."

"Child Protection probably got fooled by his wife."

"Yeah, she was nice."

"Except she never stood up for us."

"You always said she was a coward."

That was true. "It pissed me off, but now I can see she was trapped herself. I'm not excusing her; she should have left and reported the bastard."

"I wonder what would have happened."

"It isn't worth looking back. We have to move forward."

"Yeah, but it's still interesting to think about it."

"It's a waste of time, nothing but chewing gum for your brain. Today and tomorrow are all that count."

"Man, between Crane and Bev, tomorrow is going to be a ginormous day."

"A top-ten one, if things work out."

Mario held up a hand. "My fingers are crossed."

"It's got nothing to do with luck. It's intention, planning, and action that make things happen."

33

―――――

Laura, wearing a Kiss T-shirt I bought at a concert twenty years ago, sauntered into the kitchen.

"Good morning. You're up early."

I was taking a pod out of the drawer for my second cup. "Morning, you want coffee?"

"Yes, please. You were up all night."

"I know, I just couldn't fall asleep."

She pecked my cheek. "You have too much on your mind."

"Who doesn't?"

"Come on, you're thinking about Bev. It's natural."

As the coffee streamed into her mug, I said, "It might be rough for a while, but I have a feeling she'll be all right."

"When are you going to tell Dawn?"

"I keep ping-ponging it. She should know, but then she's going to want to see her, and if Bev is all screwed up, it could backfire."

"If you don't say something now, when would you?"

I handed her a mug of coffee. "When Bev gets out of rehab."

She took a sip and sat down. "What about telling Bev you found Dawn and she has a grandchild?"

"I don't know what to do. I thought I should ask the rehab place what they thought, but then I realized the situation is so crazy, nobody would know what to do."

"Why would you think that?"

"Because Bev was in foster care, got left behind, became an addict and prostitute, then left her kid, who became homeless, is that enough?"

"I know it's complicated, and you're never going to find someone with the exact same circumstances, but all these 'things,' are forms of trauma."

"Did you take classes in this stuff?"

"I minored in psychology, but I learned a lot by reading."

"Do you think I should ask the rehab place?"

"At least talk to them about both situations. They'll have ideas on how to handle it."

I was sure they did, but I was the one who'd have to live with the fallout if they were wrong.

"I'm thinking we should tell Dawn we found Bev. She knew we were looking for her and that she was into drugs and all."

Laura said, "True. But keep in mind the reality of finding her is different than searching for her."

"I'm going to wait until Bev is in rehab."

"Okay."

"As far as Bev knowing about Dawn and her granddaughter, maybe I'll ask the rehab people."

"Good idea, maybe they'll think it'll help motivate her to kick her habit."

That was true, but seeing her daughter and granddaughter and learning they were homeless would remind her of her failure as a mother. It could drive her to lose herself in drugs or worse.

There was only one other shopper in the cereal aisle. I put two boxes of Raisin Bran in my cart and pulled out the new burner phone I'd bought. I logged onto Publix's open Wi-Fi network. As the lone shopper rolled out of the aisle, I navigated to the first social media site that allowed adult content and logged in under an alias.

I attached five images to a new post and typed a headline to go with it: *Atlas Crane kills his wife and now this?*

There was no need to be worried about a defamation suit coming from Crane because he did it.

Before hitting send, I set up copies of messages to be posted on three other social media sites. Smiling, I unleashed them on the internet.

Using the express checkout lane, I paid for my cereal and drove straight to my house. I pulled into the garage and checked the first site I'd posted on.

I blinked. The numbers were huge: two thousand views, a hundred and ten comments, and almost a thousand shares. It was spreading faster than a kindergarten cold.

The engagement at the other sites I'd posted were similar. I navigated back to the original site. Every time I refreshed the screen the numbers leapt higher.

Using my regular cell phone, I took a picture of the screen and made a call.

"Detective Moreno."

"Hey, Moe, I got something you need to see."

"What's up?"

"The guy who tipped me off about Atlas Crane and his involvement in porn just sent me a post."

"What's the nature of the post?"

"Hold on, let me text you a screenshot of it."

"Okay."

"You get it?"

"It just came in. Jesus Christ! This guy is a sick bastard."

"You got that right."

Moreno said, "And he had the balls to deny it. I hate to say it, but I almost bought it."

"I was told this came from his phone, and there is more on the phone and his laptop."

"We won't have a problem getting a warrant now."

"That's good. How long do you think it'll be before you search his home?"

"A day or so."

"If you need any more proof, check adult sites like MeWe, Reddit, Pictoa, and Bluesky."

"Geez, how many sites are there?"

"Too many, if you ask me."

"You got that right. Let me get going with this."

"Keep me posted."

I ran the rest of the plan through my head. It had a good chance of working, and now was the time to see if it would.

34

———

I GAVE A QUICK SECOND TO THE IDEA OF HAVING A CUP OF coffee and passed. There was enough adrenaline coursing through my system. Instead, I grabbed a bottle of water from the fridge and went into the den.

Sitting at my desk, I used a burner to send a message to Atlas: *I warned you. Confess or it gets even worse.*

Before hitting send, I attached a screenshot of the post that was swamping the internet.

Using my laptop, I altered the pornography image, adding black boxes over any faces and private parts. Satisfied it was suitable for Facebook, I used an alias account and spread the post into seven Naples groups.

I had to run to Fort Myers that evening to pick up Bev, but it would have been nice to enjoy what I'd set in motion. I grabbed a lululemon bag out of the closet and transferred the cash I'd hidden beneath the sink.

I put the bag into a backpack and put it under the desk. It was time to check in with Atlas. I dialed his number, and he answered on the fifth ring.

"Sorry, Beck."

"Hey, Atlas, if it ain't a good time, you can call me back."

"No, it's not that. My phone has been blowing up with calls."

"Why's that?"

He hesitated. "There's a ton of shit going around the internet about me."

"You? I don't understand."

"Whoever is trying to force me to confess to killing Ana is putting porn out, saying it came from me."

"Pornography?"

"Yeah, and if you can fucking believe it, it looks like child porn."

"Yikes. Oh now I see why the police did the raid and—"

"I got nothing to do with that stuff. I swear."

"Child pornography is as nasty as I gets."

"I know, it's disgusting."

"You have to deal with this as fast as possible. This stuff gets around, it's going to get rough for you. People get crazy. You have a gun?"

"Yeah. Why?"

"You have to be careful. People lose their minds with this kind of stuff and do stupid things."

"You got to see some of the comments on the posts; it's filled with threats."

"That's what I'm talking about, all it takes is one guy with a screw loose. A nutjob thinks he'd be some kind of hero by taking out a predator. Keep your eyes open."

"You think someone would come after me? I didn't do anything."

"If I were you, I'd think seriously about finding someplace else to stay until this thing blows over."

"Really? I can't believe this shit."

"I hate to break the news to you, but it's probably going to get bad, real bad."

"How can it get worse than it is?"

"You said the stuff on social media is pretty new, right?"

"Yeah, why?"

"The more people find out about what they're saying about you, the higher the chance of something happening. The media is going to get on it, and your friends, I mean, your neighbors are going to freak out."

"This is so fucked up! I didn't do anything. I'd never mess with that shit. I'm not some creepy weirdo."

"I know, but unfortunately, at this point, it doesn't matter. People are going to judge you on whatever the post says. It's sad, but that's the world we live in."

"Somebody just rang the bell."

"I wouldn't answer it."

"Why?"

"Because people are crazy."

"This shit has got to end."

"Hey, Laura is calling, I've got to pick her up. I'll check back with you later."

I switched calls, but it wasn't Laura calling.

It was Atlas's son, Tyler Crane.

"Hey, Tyler."

"Did you do this?"

"Do what?"

"Spread this garbage about my father? He's a lot of things, but he's not a pedophile."

"Hold on a sec—"

"I can't believe you did something like this. Sexual deviancy is way out of bounds."

"Look, you asked me to get justice for your mother, and I agreed. I warned you it would get rough, and you said it was okay. I think your exact words were to do whatever you have to."

"Well, that was a mistake, and I want you to stop. Now."

"It's too late for that."

"No, it's not. I'll go to the—"

"Look, you're panicking for no reason. Once you know how this is going to play out, you'll be on board."

"So, tell me how you're going to fix this."

35

Driving north on Route 75, I went over the checklist in my head. It felt like something was missing. Laura had gone overboard getting Bev the clothes she'd need for rehab. The wheely was in the trunk along with books, makeup, and healthy snacks.

Bev was probably a smoker, but I'd wait until I knew what brand she smoked. I passed the airport and exited. I navigated my way to the bar Igor owned, wondering if Bev was inside.

In case we needed a quick getaway, I backed into a space near the entrance. Lifting my left pant leg, I checked the holster and covered it. Grabbing another pistol from the glove box, I stuck it in the waistline at the small of my back.

Taking a deep breath, I took the backpack out of the passenger footwell, got out of the car, and headed to the door.

I stepped aside as a man stumbled out of the bar. He was mumbling in Russian. Entering the bar, I paused, and the room came into focus. Four young men, all with shaved heads and tattoos, were around a table anchored by a bottle of vodka. Two groups of older men, including some I'd run into on my first visit, were seated at the bar.

The place quieted with all eyes on me as I stepped further in.

Going up to the bartender, the only sound was the buzzing from a neon sign above the bar.

"I'm here to see Igor."

"He isn't here."

"I have an appointment with him."

"Like I said, Igor isn't here."

"Come on. Tell him I'm here."

Putting two hands on the bar, the barkeeper said, "He hasn't been here all day."

"He's supposed to meet me."

He spoke to the other bartender in Spanish, and the other man said, "All we know is he ain't here. Come back tomorrow, he might be here."

"Look"—I raised the backpack—"I got something for him. Call him, tell him Beck is here."

A pair of the shaved heads came over. "What do you want?"

"I'm not here for trouble. Igor said he would meet me tonight to get this."

"What is it?"

"Call him and tell him Beck is here."

"What's in the bag?"

I backed up. "Money. It's Igor's. Now call him before I leave and tell him you didn't want the cash."

The shaved-heads talked in Russian to each other. One pulled out a phone and made a call. He spoke in Russian.

He put his hand over the phone. "What is your name?"

"Beck. Tell him I'm here."

He went back to speaking Russian and ended the call.

"Igor is in Tampa. He said come back tomorrow."

The other shaved heads seated at the table got up and left.

I said, "Are you shitting me?"

"That's what he said."

"Did he say anything about Bev?"

"Come back tomorrow."

"Call him back. I need to talk to him."

"Igor is busy."

"Where in Tampa is he?"

"I don't know." He waved to the door. "Go. Go home now."

I hoisted the backpack on and slid the gun from the small of my back to the right of my belly button. I took two steps backward before turning around.

Swinging the door open, I drew my pistol and stepped to the right. As the door closed, the two shaved heads who left appeared.

Pointing my gun, I said, "Back off or I'll kill you both."

"Give us the money."

I stepped away. "Get back inside."

"Igor said to get the money. Give it up."

The door opened and the other shaved heads appeared.

I put a hand on my car and found the door handle. "I don't want any trouble, but if *you* do, I'll kill you. So, don't make a move."

I opened the door, "Get inside! Or I'll shoot your frigging kneecaps off!"

As I pointed the pistol at their legs, they backed off. I jumped in the car and peeled out of the lot.

Driving home, I wondered where Bev was. Was Igor really tied up, or had he tried to scam me?

Before getting on the highway, I called Mario and updated him.

He said, "Damn it!"

"I don't know if Igor had any intention of being there."

"He's no Boy Scout, but we've always been able to work with him."

Getting on the entrance ramp, I said, "Yes, but this felt like it could've been a setup."

"It'd be crazy for him to burn a bridge like us. I'm going to talk to a few people, see what I can find out."

"All right. I'm going to call the rehab place to let them know she's not coming tonight."

"Okay. We'll talk later."

I dialed Laura. She answered on the first ring.

I said, "Hey, how's it going?"

"What happened?"

"She wasn't there."

"What happened?"

I told her Igor hadn't shown up and left out the part where they tried to steal the forty grand I was carrying.

"I'm sorry."

"It's okay. We're going to try to set up another handoff."

"When?"

"Hopefully tomorrow."

"You have to call Oasis Recovery—"

"I did already."

"How are you feeling about it?"

"About what?"

"Not getting Bev. I know you had your hopes up."

"I'm okay."

"It's normal to be disappointed."

"I'm not disappointed."

"I can hear it in your voice, but if you want to play macho—"

"I'm a little bummed, but we'll see what happens tomorrow."

"It's good to express your emotions. Get it out of your system, it makes things better."

"Emotions don't make things better, what does is taking action. This isn't over, we'll get her."

36

———————

My cell rang. It was one of the guys we used for small, nonconfidential jobs.

"Yo, Beck. I'm here. It's a crazy scene. A news truck just pulled up."

"WINK News?"

"Yep, they're here."

"Perfect. FaceTime me. But don't use my name when you're talking."

"Truth. Standby."

I shut my camera off, and the live stream from the scene in front of Atlas Crane's house appeared on my iPad.

He panned the crowd. There must have been thirty or forty people gathered in the street. About a dozen of them were holding signs. I took a screenshot and said, "What do the signs say?"

The shaky video footage settled on a gray-haired woman holding a white poster board. The handwritten message read, *You're sick Atlas Crane. Get out of our neighborhood.*

"Let me see another one."

My proxy said to a protester, "Hey, mister. Do you mind if I show my bud your sign?"

The man had a bodybuilder physique and said, "Go for it."

We'll get you Atlas, you pervert.

"Check this one out."

A pair of grandmotherly women held the ends of a sign stating, *Keep our kids safe. Lock up all sex offenders forever!*

I took another screenshot and asked, "Is there anything going on inside the house?"

"Hang on a sec. You gotta see this."

He swung the video feed to a pair of blonde girls standing in front of what had to be their mothers. The little kids were holding a sign written in crayon. It read, *Please protect us from people like Atlas Crane.*

"Make sure the news people get these kids on camera. What about the house?"

The phone shakily moved closer to Crane's home. "All the shades are down, but check out what's on the garage."

"I can't read it. Can you zoom in?"

"Some dude spray painted 'Pedophile' on the garage door."

It was going better than I hoped. "Okay. Let's get off the call and make sure you don't talk to anyone, especially any reporters."

After FaceTime ended, I placed a call to my contact at WINK News. They were going to run the story no later than 5 p.m., and she said it would be shown on each of the night's broadcasts.

I told her to keep someone at the Crane house all the time. She asked why, and I said she had to trust me.

It was time to call Atlas's son, Tyler. Before I called, I sent a text with the screenshots of the protesters and their signs. He picked up on the first ring.

"Who are these people?"

"Neighbors and concerned citizens."

"This is worse than I thought, we can't—"

"You need to go see your father. He's under a lot of pressure. He might be willing to confess to murdering your mother."

"This is surreal, I never should have got you involved."

"It's going to be okay."

"How can you say that? His reputation, my family name is garbage. The stigma will never go away. I'm going to have to move, maybe change my name, it's a mess. I—"

"Tyler, go see your father before it gets worse."

"How can it get worse than this?"

"The police will probably search his house."

"And they're going to find more stuff? I can't—"

"Go see your father! If he confesses now, we'll unwind all this."

The doorbell rang. Through the window I could see it was Mario.

"Hey, come in."

We embraced and Mario said, "I was able to find out Igor is going to be in Fort Myers today. He should be there by four, I was told."

"Are you sure?"

"Yeah, I got it from two different people."

"What about Bev? Is she going to be there?"

He shook his head. "I couldn't confirm that. She could be, uh, working up there."

"What about them trying to rob me? Any info on whether Igor was involved in that?"

"I don't know. Nobody seemed to know what happened, but they're all tight-lipped. Igor doesn't take leaks lightly."

"If it was Igor, the game has changed. We can't be working with the Russians any longer."

"It could be him. Remember when he backdoored the Cubans?"

"That was payback for one of Santos's guys ratting about the stolen cars Igor was running through Miami."

"Really? Who told you that?"

"You should come with me to pick up Bev."

"Sure."

"If Igor is playing it straight with us, Bev has to be in the area."

"You're right. What time do you want to go?"

"Let's leave around seven. If it goes well, we'll drop Bev at the rehab before eight."

I waited in a visitor's parking spot diagonally across the street from Tyler Crane's coach home. I put the *Practical Stoicism* podcast on. Pondering a piece on Marcus Aurelius Meditations on inner peace, the garage door on Tyler's unit lifted.

As he pulled into his garage, I shut off the podcast and sent him a text message. He closed the garage door and walked across the street.

I opened the passenger door. Tyler got in and I asked, "How did it go with your father?"

"It was a mess. All his neighbors were in the street. They were screaming at me when I went into the house. I really think somebody is going to try and hurt him."

"What did he say? Is he going to confess?"

"He doesn't want to."

"Of course he doesn't. But if he wants this nightmare to end, he's going to have to."

"I feel bad for him."

"He killed your mother. Keep reminding yourself of that."

"I know, but this pedophile stuff is . . ."

"What did you say to him?"

"I told him to tell the truth, that I knew he killed Mom, and that if he did, this child pornography stuff would go away."

"You said it just like that?"

"Yes, but he still wouldn't confess."

"That's okay. He'll get there soon."

"What makes you believe that?"

"Things are going to heat up."

"Are you kidding me?"

"I've got to run up to Fort Myers, but stay in touch with your father. See if he changes his mind about confessing."

"It doesn't look like he's going to."

"He will. I gotta go. I'll be in touch."

The way I figured it, Atlas knew he was in deep trouble. His hope that things would clear up needed one more shove to disappear.

37

―――――

MARIO JOGGED DOWN THE DRIVEWAY OF HIS CONDO AND HOPPED in my BMW.

"Man, it's so humid out."

"It needs to rain."

Mario clicked his seat belt on. "This is so cool. I can't believe were going to save Bev."

"Getting her out of the hands of these bastards is one thing. It's the saving part that worries me."

"Trust me, I know kicking her habit ain't going to be easy for her."

"She's going to need counseling for a long time."

"That's what Susan said. She said the drugs are one thing, but abandoning your child and selling yourself are going to be tough to deal with."

Had Susan and Laura talked about this, or were females better in tune with mental trauma?

"Right now, we get her into recovery and go from there. One day at a time."

"As long as Igor isn't jerking us around, this should be a one-two-three thing."

With more confidence than I felt, I said, "We have to be prepared, but I'm not expecting any more trouble."

"Me neither. So, is everything set with Atlas?"

"The wheels are in motion. I can tell you, if this was anything other than picking up Bev, I would've canceled it."

"I can't believe we're going to miss one of the best parts of this job."

"I know, but I just hung up with Katherine. She's going to send over the video. "

"So, we'll get a highlight reel?"

"More than that, I asked her to send me everything they shot."

"Cool. We have something to look forward to watching."

I waited a beat before saying, "I'm getting worried about the kid, Tyler."

"What's going on?"

"He didn't appreciate the incentive to make his old man come clean."

"That's the price of admission."

"We know it, but Tyler is making noise."

"What's he going to do? Go to the cops?"

I reminded him, "We can't have any publicity."

"Do you want me to talk to him?"

"No. I've got it handled. If it looks like it'll get hairy, I've got an ace to use."

"Always prepared, aren't you?"

"Yes, and speaking of being prepared, let's go over the plan for when we get to Igor's."

We ran through several scenarios and wound our way to Igor's Royal Silk Bar and Grill.

I reversed into a space near the entrance.

"There's a back door in the room where I met Igor the first time."

"You told me already."

"Okay. Remember, keep the front door open and stay off to the side."

"I got it."

"And make sure your pistol is visible."

"Yes, Daddy."

Reaching toward the back seat, I grabbed the backpack filled with money. "All right, let's get Bev."

The humidity was as high as the tension as we approached. I swung open the door. Mario stuck a piece of wood in between the frame and the door, preventing it from closing.

There were only three men leaning against the bar. The same four shaved heads who tried to rob me were sitting at a table playing cards. Keeping my eyes on them, I went up to the bartender.

"Tell Igor Beck is here."

The barkeeper ducked under the bar and knocked on the door to the rear room. He cracked open the door and stuck his head in. A second later he waved to me. "Come over here. He's ready to see you."

Nodding to Mario, I went into the room where Igor held court. The Russian was sitting behind a desk, and to his left stood a man in sunglasses who was stretching the seams on the sweat suit he wore.

Igor's eyes zeroed in on the backpack. He grinned. "Beck, now we meet after so long time."

"I was here a day ago."

"It was a mix-up. But you are here now with Igor."

Eyeing the muscleman, I said, "Where is Bev?"

"You are all business." He reached behind for a bottle of vodka on a credenza. "Have a drink first."

"No, thanks."

"Sit. Igor will have one."

He poured himself a shot glass of vodka and threw it back.

"I didn't appreciate your goons trying to rip me off the other night."

He tilted his head. "Igor doesn't understand, tell Igor."

"The group of chrome domes playing cards tried to rob me."

His expression was difficult to read. He said something in Russian, and the hulk got up. I put my hand on the gun in my pocket and the muscleman left the room.

"We've worked together a long time, Igor, and I thought we respected each other."

"Yes, Igor respect Beck."

The door opened. I jumped to my feet as the leader of the shaved-head contingent walked in.

"Easy, Beck. Igor want to know the truth."

Igor got up, and the hulk put his hand on the shaved head's shoulder, forcing him to sit. Igor circled the desk, sitting on the edge of it. He spoke in Russian. The bald man shook his head and mumbled.

Igor yelled at him, and the shaved head turned to me and said, "I'm sorry. We were out of line."

I nodded as Igor swiped the bottle of vodka off the desk. He cracked the bottle over the bald man's head. Blood streamed down his forehead.

Igor spoke in Russian and his muscleman grabbed the bleeding man under his armpit and escorted him out of the room.

Shaking his head, Igor said, "It is difficult to get good men these days."

"I've got the money. Where is Bev?"

"Good. She is working close by."

"Where?"

He beckoned with his hand, "You pay, you get her."

"This better not be a scam."

"Igor always keep his word. Without word, we got nothing. No, Beck?"

I reached into the backpack and took out the money. I stacked it on his desk. Igor fanned through four of the packs and nodded.

He spoke to his henchman in Russian and stood. "Okay. Boris will take you to her."

38

I LEFT THE ROOM AND LOOKED AT MARIO, WHO WAS ON GUARD by the front door. I gave him a thumbs-up and his stance relaxed.

"Where's Bev?"

I hiked a thumb at the muscular Boris and said, "Schwarzenegger is going to take us to her."

"Where are we going?"

"Igor said it's close by."

Boris said, "Follow me."

The Russian climbed into a black Escalade, and we followed him out of the parking lot.

I swiped away a second call from Tyler and told Mario that Igor had broken a bottle over the leader of the guys who tried to rob me.

"So, Igor wasn't behind it then."

"I don't think so."

"Going rogue isn't the best strategy when you're working for Igor."

"I know, it doesn't make sense."

"But there's no fixing stupid."

"Amen. He's turning."

We pulled into the parking lot for a two-story motel whose better days were when Kennedy was president.

The Russian pulled into a space in front of a room. Sitting on a folding chair in front of the room was a fat man mopping his face with a rag.

As I parked, Mario said, "I can't believe it. We really found her."

My stomach knotted. "It's crazy. Come on."

The Russian pointed at us, and the overweight man knocked on the door to the room he was guarding. I pushed the thought Bev was servicing a client out of my head.

Chubby opened the door and said, "Get out here!"

My eyes shot between the door and the two men.

He yelled into the room, "Come on, we don't have all damn day!"

I inched forward, "I got this."

I whispered to Mario, "Stay here and be on your toes."

Stepping into the room, I said, "Bev? It's Beck and Mario. You're safe now."

The furniture was scuffed and had been there since the motel had opened. A bed took up most of the space in the dark room.

The bedspread was pulled down on one side and a pillow dented. A can of Coke was on the nightstand. On the floor was a white leather jacket. An embroidered patch of a pair of ballerina slippers was sewn onto the side showing. It was the jacket Bev had worn in the picture Mario had gotten from the Albanians.

I picked it up. There was a streak of blood on the waistband. I dropped it.

"Bev, are you in the bathroom? Is everything all right?"

To the right of a section with a rod full of empty hangers

was the bathroom. The door was closed. At the bottom of the door was a band of yellow light.

I knocked. "Bev?"

No reply. An image of her lying in a bathtub with her wrists slashed careened into my head. I pushed it out and pounded on the door.

"Bev! It's Beck and Mario. You're going home."

There was no answer. The door was locked. I pulled my arm into my chest and rammed the door with a shoulder. The door splintered.

The bathroom looked empty. I pushed aside the shower curtains. Nothing but an empty tub with a scum line. My gaze went to the open window.

I grabbed Bev's jacket and flew out of the room. "She left through the window." I ran toward the rear of the motel. "Hurry! Around the back."

I turned around the corner of the building. Surveying the first-floor windows, I ran to the open one. The hedge line under the window was flattened. Several branches had been snapped in half.

I studied the parking lot as Mario and the Russian arrived. Two dumpsters were in a corner of the lot. I ran toward them. "Bev! It's Beck. You're safe. I just want to talk."

Circling the trash bins, I lifted both tops and pulled back from the stench. The parking lot backed up to a street. I looked both ways but there was no trace of her.

"Come on. We have to look for her."

We hopped in the BMW, and I drove straight to the street running behind the motel.

Mario said, "Are you sure she was there?"

"I found her jacket, the one in the photo you got from the Albanians."

"Maybe it was planted by Igor."

I hadn't considered that. "You think so?"

"I don't know, but it's a possibility."

"If he screwed us out of forty grand, he's got to know we'd come after him."

"Yeah, but why would she run?"

"She's scared."

"Of us?"

"The whole thing. Bev's been passed around, she probably thought it was happening again."

"Didn't Igor tell her we were getting her?"

"I don't know, but would you believe it?"

"Yeah, I guess you're right."

"Look at her jacket, there's blood on it."

"Blood?" He grabbed it off the back seat and examined it.

"She better be all right."

I pulled to the curb. "Ask that guy if he's seen her."

Mario jumped out of the car and went up to a man sitting on the steps of a house. The man shook his head and Mario came back. "Said he didn't see anybody, but I think he was lying."

I banged the steering wheel with the palm of my hand. "We'll look around some more, then we're going to see Igor."

Half an hour later, we were back at the bar. We walked in and headed straight for the back room. A bartender shouted, "Hey, you can't go back there."

I knocked and threw open the door. Igor was on the phone.

"Where is she?"

Igor frowned and ended the call. "What is the matter?"

"Bev wasn't in the room your goon took us to."

"That is strange."

"Are you fucking with us?"

"Igor make deal, Igor keeps up his end."

"Well, your end is hanging in the wind."

Igor made a call and spoke in Russian. He hung up.

"She was there, but she ran." He shrugged. "They always try to get away."

"I want my money back."

"If Igor find her, she will pay."

"You can't hurt her!"

"It is the only way to teach her a lesson."

"Did she try to run away before?"

"They all try."

"Her jacket had blood on it. What happened?"

"Igor doesn't know."

"Ask your men."

"They don't know."

"How would you know without checking with them?"

"Igor knows everything."

"Yeah? Well, where is she?"

"Igor will find her, but you will pay Igor's expenses."

"That's bullshit. You didn't deliver your end of the deal."

"Igor will look around."

"I want her found, and fast."

Igor glared at me and sat but said nothing.

We got back in my car and Mario said, "I don't trust that bastard."

"Trust is bullshit, okay? If you depend on trust to get things done, you're deluding yourself. What matters is how someone benefits from something."

"Yeah? Well, we paid the bastard forty K."

"Exactly my point."

"But we didn't get Bev."

"I could be wrong, but I think Igor was caught off guard by her taking off."

"You think so? I think he's playing with us."

"It's not in his best interests to do that."

"He's got the money. Bev is probably in Jacksonville or Atlanta by now."

I hadn't thought Igor might move her to another operation in another city. "Then he's got to give us the money back."

"Good luck with that. He's got a lot of manpower, and who knows, maybe he's moving out of state or back to Russia or something."

39

———

I WALKED IN THE HOUSE AND TOBY TROTTED OVER.

Laura called out, "Beck?"

I scratched Toby's head. "Yeah."

Laura came into the family room and looked at me. "Uh-oh. What happened?"

I crumpled onto the sofa, and she put her arm around me. "Tell me what happened?"

After telling her it looked like Bev had run away. She said, "I'm so sorry."

"We're looking for her."

"You think you'll find her?"

I shrugged. "I just can't believe it."

"I know it's disappointing, and I hate to say it, but she's done this before."

Like I didn't know that. "We were so close."

"Don't give up."

I stood. "That's the last thing I'd ever do."

"I know that. If there's anything I can do to help find her, let me know."

"Thanks. I have some business to attend to."

"Oh, I forgot to tell you, on the news, they did a story on Atlas Crane. What a creep he is."

"It'll probably be on later. After I take care of what I need to, we'll watch some TV."

"Do you want me to pour you a glass of bourbon?"

"Now that sounds good."

Carrying my cocktail, I closed the den's door and opened my laptop. Clicking on Proton Mail, I navigated to my inbox. The video from my WINK News contact had come in.

I opened the message and hit play.

Over fifty people were standing in the street in front of Atlas Crane's house. The camera panned the crowd and the signs some of them held. The messages were like the ones I'd been shown on FaceTime, but the size of the gathering had grown.

The screen filled with a blonde-haired woman in her thirties.

"This is Katherine Rigby reporting live from Livingston Estates. As our viewers can see, neighbors and concerned citizens have gathered outside the home of Atlas Crane, who is suspected of having ties to child pornography. WINK News previously reported the Collier County Sheriff's Office conducted a raid, confiscating various items from a storage unit rented by Mr. Crane.

"WINK News broke the story that the unit was rented under an alias by Mr. Crane.

"Viewers may remember the name, Atlas Crane. His wife was murdered fourteen years ago, and Mr. Crane was arrested for the crime but was acquitted."

The reporter said, "Okay, let's cut here. Get a shot, make

sure it's a close-up, of the garage door. Then we'll do a couple of interviews."

The cameraman said, "Okay. I got it, let's move on."

The reporter brushed her blonde hair behind her ears and smiled into the camera. "Mr. Crane's neighbors became furious when the allegations became public. We'd like you to hear from a few of them."

The camera cut to a woman in her forties holding a sign reading: *Protect Our Children!*

"This is Tracy Mulligan, who lives across the street. Mrs. Mulligan, why are you out here protesting?"

Face pinched with disgust, the woman said, "We don't want pedophiles or sexual deviants in our neighborhood. I heard they found sick pictures in his storage unit. My kids play out here. They have a right to be kept safe and away from creeps like him."

"Have you ever witnessed Mr. Crane exhibiting any behaviors that concern you?"

The crowd gathered behind the woman grew.

"You know, I never thought much about it in the past, but he was always lurking around, watching the kids play. He makes me sick. You had to see the way he looked at them. You could see his evil mind working, you know what I mean?"

"What would you like to see happen?"

"He should be in jail and the key thrown away. I mean, damn it, he killed his wife, and now this? Why the hell isn't he behind bars already?"

The reporter nodded and the camera moved to a man in his sixties wearing a baseball cap. "Sir, can we ask what brought you out here today?"

In a New York accent, the man said, "When he got off from killing his wife, I said maybe he's not guilty and deserves a second chance, but now, with the filth they found in his storage locker? Something's got to be done. I have three grandkids, seven, nine, and ten years old. Me and my wife watch them every day after school."

"What do you think should be done about it?"

"Where I come from, if the police don't handle it, we would."

The reporter said, "As you can see, tensions are high. We're waiting for the sheriff's office to respond to our request for— hold on a second, it looks like there's a development."

As the camera viewpoint shifted, sirens could be heard. Two patrol cars were coming down the street.

As the crowd parted, the reporter said, "The police are here. Let's see if they'll comment."

The video feed bounced as the reporter approached the officers.

"Excuse me, Officer."

A uniformed officer brushed past the reporter and the camera followed him and three other cops to the front door of Crane's home.

The reporter said, "They're not here to disperse the crowd. The police are knocking on Atlas Crane's door. I can hear them instructing him to open the door. The door remains closed despite the pleas of the officers. One officer is holding up a document. He said they're here to execute a search warrant."

The door opened, Crane was shown the warrant, and the officers entered the home. The crowd surged toward the house. A man in his thirties began chanting, "Lock him up! Lock him up!" Within ten seconds the crowd joined him.

I paused the video. It was time to call Tyler back.

He answered, saying, "I called you ten times."

"I'm sorry, but I was tied up in Fort Myers."

"They're searching my father's house."

"I heard. It's the perfect time to tell him to confess."

"I already called him. He said no way. He said the cops won't find anything."

"That's the wrong decision."

"I don't care anymore, I just want this over with. If he gets away with murder, I'll just have to let it go."

"Meet me for lunch at EJ's in Bayfront. How about one o'clock?"

"Lunch? With everything that's going on?"

"We can talk it over."

"I don't see the point of meeting. We have to end all of this."

"Trust me, I realize it's tough, but you need to hang in there just a little longer. The end is near."

"I don't know."

"Look, you're paying me a lot of money to help you, and I'm going to get you what you paid for. We're just about done. I'll explain the last part to you tomorrow."

"People are starting to talk about me, and I had nothing to do with anything."

"Once your father confesses, and he will soon, all the other stuff will go away."

"How can you be so sure? He said he'd never confess."

"Because I know. You'll see tomorrow."

40

—————

THE SUN WAS PEEKING OVER THE TOPS OF THE TREES WHEN Laura came into the kitchen. "Good morning. You're up early."

"I couldn't sleep."

"I know, you were tossing and turning all night."

"Sorry."

"It's okay. I know you're worried about what happened with Bev."

"I just hope she's safe."

"I hope you realize there's a chance she just doesn't want to be found."

"That doesn't make sense. Why would she want to continue living the shitty life she is?"

"I'm just saying, maybe the guilt she's feeling for walking away from Dawn, and the shame from her drug use and, uh, lifestyle is too much to bear."

"The past is the past, she's got to look forward."

"Some people aren't able to put their past behind them."

Was she talking about me? "I'm no psychologist, but we show Bev we don't give a damn about what happened, and I bet she turns her life around."

"It's going to take a lot of work."

"I've got to go."

"Where are you going, it's so early?"

"To see Larson."

The Pelican Marsh guard waved me through the gate, and I circled into a corner of the community called The Arbors. Larson's home wasn't the biggest, but my detail-oriented friend and confidant made sure it shined.

"Come in, Beck."

"Are you going to the beach today?"

"Not today. It feels like a Turkish bath with all this humidity."

"It's got to rain. It's been on the verge for three days already."

I followed him into the kitchen. "Do you want a cup of coffee?"

"No thanks, I had two already."

We sat at a kitchen table with a glass top. "I'm really sorry about what happened with Bev."

"Thanks. I guess it was too easy."

"Nothing worth fighting for ever came easy."

"That's for sure, but on this one, I don't know. I just can't shake the feeling Igor might have been playing me."

"What gives you that impression?"

"For starters, Igor has my forty grand."

Larson's eyebrows shot up. "How did that happen?"

I told him about turning over the money before going to get Bev.

He said, "I'm surprised you agreed to that."

"We've been working with him for a while."

"Wake up, Beck. He's a Russian criminal. What part about never trusting them didn't you understand?"

"But—"

Larson stood. "What were you thinking? Where was the legendary caution you talk about?"

I felt like a second-grader in the principal's office. "I'll get the money back."

"The money is irrelevant. What worries me is the fact you got lazy, or worse, you let your emotions cloud your judgment."

Did he have a point with the emotions? "That's not what happened, Ray. Igor was a source. We just used him for the Crane docs —"

"And when did you pay him for those papers?"

My chin dropped.

"You paid him when he gave them to you. Right?"

I nodded.

"I can't believe it. And this was after they tried to rob you. Didn't any bells go off?"

"I guess I let my guard down."

"That's an understatement."

"I'm going to either find Bev or get my money back."

"You don't even know if your foster sister is here."

"She is. We got a photo of her when the Albanians had her."

"Who knows when it was taken? It could have been five years ago."

"No. I know she's here. We got her jacket, the one she had on in the picture."

"I'm not sure that means anything."

"Why not?"

"The jacket and photo can be part of a scheme."

"No, that can't be."

"Really? How elaborate are the schemes you run?"

My shoulders slouched. Thoughts were pinballing in my mind.

"Even though Igor is a master counterfeiter, you never considered that, did you?"

Pushing back the chair, I said, "I have to take a leak."

I stood in front of the mirror. My cheeks were red. I'd come for help, not to get berated. I respected Larson, and what he said made me feel like crap. I screwed up. Big-time.

I flushed the toilet and turned on the faucet to buy time.

The stoics said emotions were natural, but they also said you couldn't allow them to be your master. You had to put your feelings aside, investigate and analyze before acting.

Shutting the water, I knew Larson was right. I'd taken things on face value. I looked at the bathroom window. For a moment I considered sneaking out through it. I took a deep breath and left the bathroom.

When I stepped into the kitchen, Larson said, "Are you okay?"

I nodded. "You were right. My heart got in the way."

"Normally, I'd say it was natural, but the game you're in, mistakes like that can be deadly."

"I know."

"Learn from it and move on."

"Believe me, I will. I don't want to embarrass myself again."

"That's another emotion that derails people."

"I meant that, I'm not going to let emotions get in the way, and approach everything with extreme caution."

Larson ran a fingertip around the rim of his coffee cup. "Do you realize Bev may not want to be found?"

"Yes, but that's because she's scared or embarrassed about what she did. But we'll get her the help she needs."

"And you understand that beating an addiction, one that seems to have gone on for years, is not easy?"

"It's going to be tough, but I've got to give her the shot she deserves."

"That's honorable, but make sure you don't fall into any more emotional traps."

"I know it's easy to bullshit yourself, and after all this I'm going to be on extra guard."

Larson nodded. "Let me talk to some of my contacts. It's critical we understand whether Igor is playing it straight or not."

"I really appreciate that."

Larson stood. "I hope you find her."

"Thanks."

"Today should be a big day in the Crane case. You should get going."

I followed Larson to the front door. Instead of reaching for the doorknob, he turned around and said, "I realize I was rough on you, but I had to make the point."

The one-man firing squad had made his point.

"It's okay. The reminder was needed."

Ego battered, I stepped into the sunshine. A gecko in the driveway stood on its hind legs and scampered into the bushes.

Replaying Larson's lecture, my stomach clenched. I vowed to never be in that position again.

I got in my car and took out the burner phone I used to text Atlas Crane. I typed out another message: *You're running out of time. This is your last warning, confess now!*

41

———————

I turned off Crayon Road and hit the garage door opener. As the door lifted, my phone rang. It was Detective Moreno.

"Hey, Moe. What's happening?"

"Just a quick call to let you know they're on the way."

"Great. Have a good one."

"You too."

I walked into the house. Exhaling, I dumped my keys into the bowl on the table. Toby barked. He was out back.

Laura looked over her laptop. "What's wrong?"

"Nothing."

"What did Larson have to say?"

"Not much."

"Why did you go there, then?"

I opened a slider and Toby bolted in. "Just some business, that's all."

"You told him about what happened with Bev?"

Dismissing the urge to tell her no, I said, "Yes. He is going to make some calls to see if he can help."

"What does he think of what went on?"

I loved her, but the rapid-fire questions were a problem. "He said to be careful."

"That's all?"

"Yes. Why are you harping on it?"

"Because you look like a puppy dog who just got yelled at for peeing on the floor."

"What are you talking about?"

"What did he say about the money?"

"What money?"

"The money you paid to get Bev."

I hesitated. "I don't know what you're talking about."

"You told me you were paying to get her back from the people pimping her."

"So?"

"What happened to the money?"

Rather than lie, I walked into the kitchen and took a bottle of water out of the fridge.

"He couldn't have been happy to know you didn't get the money back."

"What are you talking about?"

She got up and went into the kitchen.

"You took the money, which was under the sink and in your backpack. When you came home that night, you left your backpack out. It was lying around all night. If it was filled with money, you would have hidden it."

And right there was the downside to having her move in permanently. "It's not what you think. The money isn't lost."

"I didn't say it was, but you didn't get what you paid for, right?"

"Look, I don't need this right now, okay? First Larson, and now you?"

"Oh. Now I see. He wasn't pleased about it."

My phone rang. I dug it out. It was Tyler Crane. I swiped it away.

"For your information, we didn't talk about the money."

"What was he mad about?"

"He wasn't mad. He just wanted to make sure I didn't let my emotions get in the way when dealing with this whole Bev thing."

"What did he say?"

"Look, I don't feel like rehashing it, okay?"

The phone rang again. It was Tyler. Again. I swiped it away.

I walked out of the room. "I have to deal with this."

Sitting behind my desk, I tapped a text out to Tyler: *I know all about it. We'll deal with it at lunch.*

A second later, my phone rang. It was Tyler. I swiped it away and sent another text: *At the doctor's and can't talk. I'll see you later.*

Call me when you're done.

It was best not to respond.

I heard Laura call out, "I'm going to Publix. Do you need anything?"

"No. Nothing special."

"Okay."

I waited five minutes before leaving the den for the family room. I flicked the TV on and bounced between channels looking for the news.

Nothing but a bunch of daytime talk shows and poorly acted soaps. I grabbed Toby's leash. "Come on, boy."

He ran to me and sat. I put his leash on, and we headed out for a walk.

Toby sniffed around like it was the first time he'd been in the neighborhood. We headed left, and seeing the preserve brought me back to the night he found Dawn and her baby.

It was hard to imagine the turn my life had taken: Laura was basically living with me, Dawn and her kid were dependents, reuniting with Bev became a reality, and I'd handed over forty grand with nothing to show for it.

Except for the money, everything was positive, but a blue feeling overshadowed them.

I tugged Toby away from a frog who'd been crushed by a car, knowing the real reason for the funk. The bottom line was being reprimanded by Larson.

I knew he was right, but disappointing Larson felt bigger, almost betrayal-like. My respect for him had nothing to do with the success he'd achieved. It was genuine. He'd had a good marriage before losing his wife to cancer and had fathered a son who was a good man and successful in his own right.

I relied on bouncing things, both personal and professional, off Larson. I told him things I wouldn't say to Mario. He was more than a father figure. If Larson thought less of me, it would ruin our relationship.

———

I slid into a space on Bayfront's main drag. Tyler was pacing the sidewalk in front of EJ's Café. He walked toward me.

"They arrested my father!"

I raised a finger to my lips. "Shush."

Tyler looked in both directions, focusing on a woman pushing a stroller. The lady made a U-turn and headed across the street.

Patting his shoulder, I said, "Let's have a quick lunch."

"How can you eat at a time like this?"

"Come on, you need to eat."

"I don't want to eat."

I headed to the café, and he followed.

I picked a table in the rear of the outdoor section and guided him to a chair.

"Where'd they take him?"

"Probably the county jail."

"He needs a lawyer."

"He does. Do you have anyone in mind?"

"I don't know any lawyers. Do you?"

"Don't worry, I'll hook this up. I know a ton of attorneys."

"He needs a good one, the best."

I raised a palm as the server came over.

I said, "I'll have a jalapeno burger. Medium well."

Tyler said, "I don't want anything."

"Bring him a turkey panini. If you don't eat it, you can take it home."

The server left, and Tyler said, "I told you this whole thing was a mistake, and you kept saying it would work out, and now he's in jail."

"Look, you came to me about your father getting away with murdering your mom. There's no doubt he did it. He's a murderer."

"I know, but now these crazy child porn charges you pinned on him, they're worse. They tried to burn his house down. They'll attack him in jail. He may not survive the night."

Leaning forward, I said, "He's got the perfect incentive to confess."

"If he does, you'll get rid of all this porno stuff?"

"Yes. He'll be where he belongs."

"Okay."

"He'll be arraigned in the morning. At that time, he should be released on bail, and we'll deal with everything."

"How can you be sure?"

"I spoke with a couple of lawyers. He owns the house, and

though he was on trial before, he doesn't have a record. They should let him out."

"What if they don't?"

"They will. He may have to wear an ankle bracelet monitor. But we'll deal with it if we have to."

42

———

Toby was waiting by the interior door and jumped on me when I came in from the garage. I massaged his head, and he rolled on the ground exposing his belly.

Kneeling, I rubbed his tummy. Laura was tapping away on her laptop. The dining table was covered with papers.

I said, "Didn't you pay any attention to him?"

"I've been crazy busy. Headquarters shifted a ton of cases to us. I should make some nice money on these."

It was peanuts compared to what I'd turned over to Igor. "That's good."

She stood. "Oh, you're not going to believe it."

"What?"

"I saw on Facebook that Atlas Crane got arrested. The Naples groups are blowing up posts about it."

"For the child porn stuff?"

"Yes. Come here, I'll pull it up. It's unbelievable."

I pulled a dining chair close to Laura and sat.

"Here, look at this one. Posted in the Naples Community group."

. . .

Posted by ImaNeopolitan
DISGUSTING NEWS:

Atlas Crane, a resident of Livingston Estates, was arrested this morning on multiple counts of child pornography possession and distribution. The Collier County Sheriff's Office confirmed the arrest after an investigation that included searches of his home and a storage unit he rented.

About fourteen years ago, Crane had been put on trial for the murder of his wife. He was acquitted, but the death of a key witness during the trial may have contributed to the verdict. The case remains unsolved.

Remember to be respectful in the comments.
Comments:

- **_Susan Miner_**: *I can't believe it. He always seemed so nice. This is disgusting.*
- **_Mike The OG_**: *I knew something was off with that POS. Always too friendly with kids at the ball fields in North Collier. Lock the deviant up!*
- **_Jennifer B1962_**: *People need to calm down until all the facts are known. Innocent until proven guilty, right guys?*
- **_Robert Kline_**: *@Jennifer B1962, The facts are out. They found TONS of evidence against him. He's a sicko.*
- **_Tina the Dog Lover_**: *My heart breaks for the victims. Our kids need protection. I guess Naples isn't as safe as we think.*
- **_Sea Shells 99_**: *Oh no! I work at Mel's Diner and he used to come in all the time. He was always trying to put his hands on us.*

[Comments continue . . .]

Laura said, "The comments are coming in like mad. Let's see what the Naples Vibe group has on it."

Laura tapped her keyboard and Naples Vibe, another popular Facebook group, filled the screen. She said, "Oh my God, there's a thousand comments already."

I read the first post.

Posted by Sunny Daze

MAJOR UPDATE: Atlas Crane, the creep who got away with killing his wife, was arrested for possession of child pornography. My husband works for the Naples PD and he said the Collier Sheriff has solid evidence from Crane's computer and phone.

This sleazebag has lived here his entire life. How was he allowed to be around our children?

I'm floored. What's going on in our town?

Comments:

- **FerrariRules**: *This is insane. Burn him at the stake.*
- **RachelE.**: *I never believed he was innocent in his wife's case. Now this? He's a predator. Lock him up.*
- **DanaZ1969**: *@Rachel Evans, He was ACQUITTED. Let's not drag that up. But yeah, this new stuff is horrifying, if it's true.*
- **CarlosBuildsSandcastles**: *How does someone like this keep slipping through the cracks? First, the wife thing, now THIS? Cops need to step it up.*
- **SophiaZ**: *My heart goes out to the kids who've been exploited. This is so sad and unnecessary.*
- *[Comments continue . . .]*

Laura said, "Did you have something to do with exposing him for who he is?"

I stood. "Sometimes it takes a while, but the truth always surfaces."

"Is that a yes or a no?"

"Go back to work. I'm going to walk Toby before I take a ride."

"Where are you going?"

As soon as I opened the drawer where I kept Toby's leash, he got up. "Fort Myers."

We'd walked a block when Larson called.

"Hi, Ray."

"Hello, Beck, can you talk?"

"Sure. What's up?"

"I received some information on Igor."

I stopped dead in my tracks. "What did you find out?"

Toby tugged the leash as Larson said. "I'm hearing he's overextended."

I started walking, letting Toby lead. "In what way?"

"Igor expanded too quickly, opened up too many houses of prostitution, in too many locations, too fast, and started a gambling operation. He didn't plan properly, didn't develop the management needed, and didn't have the operating capital. It's a mistake people without management skills make, no matter the business they're in."

"He's short on cash?"

"Yes. Three of his biggest producing houses were shut down, and his second-in-command, Vladimir, went out on his own."

"He's juggling a few balls. It's a good time to press him."

"Maybe. Proceed with caution. Igor's under pressure, making him unpredictable and dangerous."

43

Paying for something and not getting it pissed most people off, including me. What made this worse was having been denied reunification with Bev.

I shouldn't have given Igor the money, but, as Larson painfully pointed out, I'd been distracted by emotion. Since I had been outnumbered, it wasn't clear how I could have forced him to give the money back.

One thing I did know was thugs detected weakness. Igor knew I was eager. Too eager. And I'd telegraphed it from the outset not only by pursuing Bev but by agreeing to overpay for her.

After Larson reamed me, I thought a lot about the situation. My biggest mistake was letting Igor know how badly I wanted to find and rescue Bev.

Mario and I did some checking, and Larson's information was right: Igor was under attack. He'd been hurt by the defection of Vladimir and the people Vladimir took with him.

A wounded animal was dangerous. With Larson's advice to proceed with caution whispering in my ear, I couldn't help feeling Igor was also vulnerable.

When he quickly agreed to meet, I took it as a good sign.

———

The traffic on Interstate 75 was heavy, giving me plenty of time to consider my decision not to have Mario come along. Igor was bound to be on edge, but being alone, I posed a lesser threat. It was his turf, but a shooting or disappearance would bring pressure from law enforcement. And heat was the last thing Igor's operations needed now.

Flickering beer signs and shaved heads were the one constant at the Royal Silk Bar and Grill. But instead of the usual four bald heads, there were only two. Had half his team of eggheads defected to Vladimir?

The place smelled of cigarette smoke. The bartenders were the same, and one of them nodded as I approached.

"I'm here to see Igor."

"Hang on."

He went to the door, knocked and stuck his head in. A second later, he waved me over. The floor in front of the bar was sticky as I made my way.

I entered the back room. Igor was running a finger across a ledger book, talking Russian to a man who wore mirrored glasses to offset the fact he was too young to shave.

They raised their heads and Igor said, "Beck, my friend. Do you want a drink?"

"No, thanks."

Igor put a pencil in the joint of the book and closed it. He dismissed the goon and said, "Igor didn't find her yet, but we are close."

"I hear you've got some big problems."

"Everyone has big problems. But you know, Igor will keep his problems instead of taking other people's problems."

"How's business?"

"Good, but can always be better, right?"

"That's not what I hear."

Igor cracked a knuckle but said nothing.

I leaned forward. "You don't have to pretend with me. We go back a long time."

"So, business is a little off. It always comes back."

"This time it's different."

"Maybe, maybe not. Nobody knows."

"I paid you forty grand for Bev. Either give me my money back, or you get me Bev."

"Igor always honors a deal."

"Give me my money back, and I'll pay you when you hand over Bev."

Igor shook his head. "Not going to happen."

"That's because you don't have the cash. And don't say you do, because I know you've got money problems."

"Every business has what you Americans call cash-flow issues."

"This can't drag on. If you can't deliver Bev in a couple of days, I want my money back."

"Igor doesn't like deadlines."

"You know I'm tight with the cops and the prosecutors' offices in both Lee and Collier. It'd be a shame if they put more heat on your operations."

He banged a fist on the table. "Don't threaten Igor."

I stood. "It's not a threat, my friend. It's a promise."

———

As soon as I got home, I called Mario.

"Hey, Beck. How'd you make out with Igor?"

I filled him in, and he said, "You told him you were going to rat out his operations?"

"I knew he couldn't deal with more shutdowns."

"But he could spill the beans on the fake Crane docs we used to rent the storage unit."

"I know, but I figure he's too distracted to open another battlefront with us."

"You're probably right."

"I need you to see what you can dig up on Vladimir. Try and see who he took with him. From what I saw, I'm getting the feeling Igor lost more than a couple of guys."

"The Albanians might have some info on it."

"They should."

Another call was coming in. It was Tyler.

"Mario, let me go, Tyler is trying to get through."

"His old man is confessing?"

"I'll let you know."

I switched calls.

After listening intently, I took my best shot at reversing what I'd heard.

Ending the call, I tossed the phone on the couch. The one thing I was sure wouldn't happen was happening. I'd planned for every contingency and never saw this happening.

What now?

I grabbed the phone and scrolled to Larson's number. Instead of dialing, I set it back on the sofa. Going to him for advice would be perceived as a sign of weakness.

Laura breezed into the house with an armful of groceries. I took two bags from her and set them on the counter.

She said, "I stopped at Whole Foods on the way back from Dawn's."

"How is she doing?"

"Pretty good, but it looks like Abby might have an ear infection or something. She has a low-grade fever."

"She needs to go to the doctor."

"Dawn is going to see what happens over the next couple of hours. If the fever gets worse, we'll get her to the pediatrician."

"Please stay on top of Dawn."

"I will. What are you doing?"

"Trying to deal with a problem."

"What kind of problem?"

"It's business."

She put her hands on her hips. "Tell me what's going on."

I wanted to tell her it was confidential, but that would set her off. "It's okay, it's delicate."

"Why don't you talk to Larson?"

I shrugged. "I should be able figure it out."

"You think he'll think less of you if you ask for help?"

She knew me too well. I wasn't sure that was a good thing. "No."

She smiled and walked down the hallway.

When the door to the bathroom closed, I picked up my phone and said, "Come on, boy. Let's go for a walk."

I didn't let Toby sniff until we were by the preserve area. It was time to make the call.

"Hey, Ray. Do you have a minute?"

"Sure, Beck. What is on your mind?"

"A situation on the Crane case came up."

"Go ahead."

"Tyler went to see his father at the county jail. Despite everything, Atlas is refusing to confess."

"You instructed the kid what to say to him?"

"Yes."

"Then it's time to talk to Atlas yourself. You're good at convincing people." He chuckled.

The compliment felt good. "I was trying to keep a low profile."

"The timing is right."

"You think so?"

Larson said, "Yes. I'm told Crane is going to be released on bail."

"Me too. His lawyer said he'd be out tomorrow."

"Wait until he's home. Call to check in on him as a friend. He can use an ally right now."

"That's for sure."

"Go work some of your famous magic on him."

I chuckled. "Thanks. I'll let you know how it goes."

After hanging up, I felt ready for the two challenges ahead.

Larson had amped me up.

The voltage then lowered considerably with the realization that Larson may have been complimenting me to make up for being rough on me.

44

———

"This is Katherine Rigby, live from the Collier County Courthouse."

The camera panned the crowd of protesters gathered in front of the court's building.

"Concerned citizens are out in force to express themselves over the impending release of Atlas Crane. Earlier today, a bail hearing was held, and Judge Whitmore agreed to release Mr. Crane on a three-hundred-thousand-dollar bond.

"WINK News has learned that Mr. Crane has put his house up as collateral. As a condition of his release, Mr. Crane must wear an ankle bracelet and stay within Collier County.

"The defense also submitted a motion to delay the trial for nine months. The prosecution objected, and Judge Whitmore was sympathetic to their arguments. He agreed to give the defense two additional months to prepare, and the trial is now on the court's calendar for January fifteenth."

The reporter was distracted by a shout, "Here he comes!"

The camera zoomed to the entrance of the building. Head down, Crane was surrounded by four men. The crowd surged toward the accused. Uniformed officers held the protesters back.

"Atlas Crane has left the court. He's being ushered to a black SUV. It looks like neither he nor his counsel will be making a statement."

The camera followed Crane as he ducked into the waiting car with his attorney. When the vehicle took off, the reporter said, "WINK News is going to continue to follow this story and update viewers with any developments."

I shut the TV, relieved that Crane had been released. Now the hard part was coming.

Going over what I was going to say to Crane when I spoke to him, my phone rang.

"Hey, Mario, Crane got out this morning."

"Cool. Look, I just heard something."

"What?"

"I'm not sure if it's a hundred percent true or not."

Why did people delay telling you what they knew? Was it a power thing?

"Spit it out, bro."

"I heard Bev went with Vladimir when he split with Igor."

"Who told you?"

"Somebody who used to work with Igor."

"Who is the somebody?"

"Remember Yenta Eddie?"

"Didn't he have a stroke a couple of years ago?"

"Yeah, almost two years now."

"What would he know?"

"He keeps in touch with the old gang. I ran into his wife at the car wash on Pine Ridge. I asked about Eddie, and she said he was keeping busy. I got his number and figured, what the hell, let me see if he knows anything. Worst comes to worst, I see how he's doing."

"That was good thinking. But you really think he knows what's going on?"

"He said everybody is watching, seeing which way this whole split goes."

"And he said Bev went with Vladimir?"

"He said Bev was tight with Vlad, and she soured on Igor because he was always trying to hook the girls on smack."

"Did he say anything about how Bev was doing? Was she using?"

"He said she was doing pretty good. She was like a manager or something."

"Do you think he's telling the truth? I don't know him well. All I remember was he never stopped talking."

"He sounded legit. But I wouldn't go all in on it."

"All right. That was super-thinking on your part."

"You think it's a good thing if she went with Vlad?"

"It's hard to say. Igor is a known thing. Vladimir was an enforcer. He'd going to have to prove himself as a leader."

"That's true. It makes him dangerous."

"He could be. I just hope Bev is okay."

"I guess she really is helping run things, you know, with the other girls."

"She's doing what she needs to survive."

"What are you thinking?"

"I'm going to see Igor again."

"You want me to come?"

"No, it's okay. I got this."

I hung up and thought about the situation with Bev and the Russians. Igor and Vlad were battling each other. That normally left an opening, but Bev was one of the pieces they were fighting over. She had moved up and was more than just an earner.

Whoever held her would not only have someone to help

manage their illicit business, it would message the street about who had the power.

45

———

THE AROMA OF GARLIC AND ONIONS PERMEATED THE AIR. I headed for the kitchen. An air fryer was on the counter, and Laura was in front of the stove sautéing something.

"That smells good. What are you making?"

"String beans."

I peered over her shoulder. "Are you sure you know what you're doing?"

"You're not the only one around here who can cook."

"What's in the fryer?"

"Chicken meatballs. Set the table, everything will be ready in five minutes."

"We're eating early like old people do."

"You said you wanted to eat by five."

"Just kidding."

After dinner, I retreated to the den and called Atlas Crane.

In a soft voice, he said, "Beck?"

"Yeah, it's me. I know things have been rough for you, and I wanted to check in on you."

He scoffed. "A shitload worse than rough."

"How are you doing, buddy?"

"Not good. My last night in jail, if it wasn't for a guard, I would've gotten my ass kicked. They had to put me in a separate cell."

"Geez. I'm so sorry."

"It's a shit show. I'm telling you, man, it's a nightmare, like I'm going to wake up and it'll be over. But it ain't."

"Damn, that's tough. I don't know how you're dealing with all this."

"I'm not. I'm trying to be positive, but I'm so down, man."

"Have you spoken to any family or friends?"

"Are you kidding? People are staying clear of me."

"That's bullshit. They weren't friends to begin with."

"I can't believe this whole thing."

"Tonight doesn't work; I'm going to be in Fort Myers, but I can come over tomorrow morning and cheer you up."

"I can use it."

"I'll see you tomorrow."

Egg-sized drops of rain pelted the windshield as I passed the Hertz Arena. Traffic slowed as my windshield wipers struggled to keep up with the water.

The downpour eased as I drove past the exit for the airport.

I exited the interstate and shook my head when I turned onto Colonial Blvd. It was bone-dry. That was Florida for you, a monsoon in one place, and half a mile away, not a drop of rain.

The parking lot of Igor's bar was empty. I counted five cars, wondering if any of them belonged to the bartenders.

I was about to pull open the door when a car door slammed. Expecting a possible ambush, I spun around. A man, carrying fifty excess pounds, was wobbling to the entrance. He took a sip of the beer he was holding. The drunk dropped the can on the pavement and crushed it with his foot.

I stuffed a scolding back in my mouth. It wasn't time to be on litter patrol, so I let it go and headed inside after the slob.

The pig waved to the bartender and made a beeline for the bathroom.

The same two shaved heads were at their usual table. Did they ever leave the place?

A lone bartender looked up from his phone and said, "What can I get you?"

Breezing past him, I said, "I'm here to see Igor."

I knocked on the door for the back room, announcing myself before opening it. Bchind his desk, Igor was on the phone. A young enforcer, hand inside his sport jacket, stepped forward.

"He's expecting me."

Sitting between two open ledger books was a stainless-steel pistol. It looked like the Sig Sauer P229 I used to own. It was a powerful 9mm pistol with a fifteen-round cartridge. Its presence and the lack of shot glasses on the desk telegraphed the jam Igor was in.

Igor finished the call, tossing his phone on the desk. He laughed. "Beck, maybe you should move to Fort Myers."

"It's not a bad ride up here, except in season."

"So, tell Igor what is on your mind."

I looked at his bodyguard. "I think it's better we talk in private."

Igor said something in Russian. The goon sneered before leaving the room.

I moved a chair closer to the desk and sat.

"I'm guessing you don't have a beat on Bev."

"The word is out. Igor will get her. You must be patient."

"Maybe I would be if you didn't have my money."

"Don't worry, Igor is honorable."

"It's not your honor that concerns me but the troubles you have now."

He scoffed. "Trouble is part of the life, nothing has changed."

I lowered my voice. "This time, it's different. Vladimir betrayed you."

His eyes narrowed. "That dog is an ungrateful bitch. Igor did so much for him. He had better watch his back."

"Vlad took a lot of your people with him. You lost a ton of manpower."

He pulled his shoulders back. "Igor still has power. You will see."

"That's not what I hear."

"So, we lose a couple of useless—"

"The guys who left were important. Vladimir was your right hand."

He picked up a pencil, saying, "Igor will be fine."

"And that thug Boris, who was always with you, he also went with Vlad."

"He was just muscle, nothing more."

"He was more than that. You had him take us to the motel. And now he's with Vladimir. That's got to hurt."

He began tapping the pencil on the desk. "Igor has seen many betrayals, but Igor is still here."

"Do you think Bev is working for Vlad?"

"Maybe she just run away."

"You know what I think? That you were set up. I think Boris took us to the motel knowing she wasn't there."

"How could he know that?"

"Because he and Vladimir arranged for her to be picked up beforehand."

Igor muttered in Russian and snapped the pencil in half.

I said, "Come on, Igor, you know she went with them. Admit it, and maybe I can help you with Vladimir."

"Tell me, how are you going to help? You don't play the same game as we do."

"That's true, but if we can weaken Vladimir, it will be good for you."

"And how do you do this?"

"We take Bev from him. She gets a few of the women in his stable to leave too."

"It is only one woman, even if five others go, it's not a big deal."

"Of course it is. Think of how it will look; anybody who might be considering leaving you for Vladimir will think twice."

He pawed his jaw.

"Plus, you get me information on where Vladimir's operations are, and I'll make sure the cops put heat, real heat, on them."

Igor smiled.

"Let's get Bev and get this started. Vladimir needs to know you're coming after what is rightfully yours."

He leaned forward, putting both elbows on the desk. "Vladimir needs a spanking. A big spanking."

"Can you find out where Bev is?"

"Igor needs a day or two."

46

———

A HANDFUL OF PROTESTERS WERE MILLING ON THE SIDEWALK IN front of Atlas Crane's house. I parked five homes away and, using the burner phone, sent a text to Crane: *Watch this. We know you did it.* I attached the video that Larson's son Tommy had enhanced for me.

A minute later, Crane replied: *I was completely acquitted.*

Confess and we'll make the pornography charges disappear.

Leave me alone!

You're going to jail anyway. At least with a clear conscious, you'll be able to sleep.

Thirty seconds later, he responded: *Go to hell!*

Before getting out of the car, I typed out a message saying he was the one going to meet Satan. I walked across the street carrying a bag of bagels.

There was no sense in antagonizing the neighbors. I sent a text to Crane, from my regular phone, telling him I was there and for him to wait by the door.

As soon as I put a foot on his walkway, the shouting began:

"What are you doing here?" "Are you a pedophile too?" "Leave our kids alone."

Crane opened the door, and I slipped inside.

"Man, are these people worked up, or what?"

"It's been a lot worse. You should've seen it when I got home yesterday. I barely made it inside."

I pointed to a shattered window. "What happened there?"

"Frigging moron threw a brick or something. Thank God, it's a hurricane window."

"There's no shortage of nutjobs out there."

"You got that right."

I handed off the bag. "I brought some bagels. They're almost as good as the ones in New York."

He got a plate and spilled the bag out.

I grabbed a sesame seeded one, tore off a piece and ate it. "Can I have some water?"

"Yeah, sure. You want coffee?"

"No, just water."

He filled a glass with Naples's finest and handed it to me.

"Aren't you going to have one?"

"I'm not hungry."

"You have to eat."

"Maybe later."

"What does your lawyer say?"

"He said if any of them step on the property, I should call the police."

"No, I mean, what does he say about the case?"

He frowned. "He said it's going to be tough, but he thinks we can win."

"Thinks?"

"I know. I have nothing to do with pornography at all. I never, ever looked at that stuff, and with little kids? Come on, I'm a father."

He was a husband as well. One who stabbed his wife to death.

"It's disgusting." I hiked a thumb toward the front of his house. "That's why they're out there."

"He's trying to get the trial moved to another county, maybe up in the Sarasota area."

"Because of the publicity?"

"Yeah."

"Have you heard from that guy who was threatening you?"

"The guy who wants me to confess to killing Ana?"

"Yes."

He picked up his phone. "The bastard sent me another text just before you got here."

"What did it say?"

"They got some bullshit video. They say it's me at the house the night Ana was killed. Said if I confessed to it, they'd make the sex charges go away."

"Wow. They can do that?"

He shrugged. "I don't know what to believe anymore."

"Did you ever consider confessing?"

"Why would I?"

He didn't say he wasn't guilty. "Because whoever is doing it looks like they set you up with the child porn stuff."

"Frigging shitheads."

"It might be the lesser of two evils."

"What?"

"Confessing to the murder."

"How can it be lesser?"

"You see all the people out there now? It'll be a zillion times worse in prison. What they do to pedophiles inside jail is . . . you know, about as gross as it gets."

He banged his fist on the table. "I'm not a goddamn pedophile!"

"It doesn't matter, what matters is that people think you are."

"We have to be able to beat these charges. They got nothing on me."

"According to the news, they've got more than enough. Plus, you don't know what else they might surprise you with at a trial."

"The news down here is biased. They've been against me from the start. That's why we're trying to move it out of Collier County."

"I hate to say it, but I don't think it's going to matter where the trial is. With social media, this stuff moves faster than the speed of light."

"It's not fair."

"You know even if you beat this, these charges are going to stick with you. A trial is going to be publicized like crazy. People who don't know about it will find out about it, and your reputation is going to be damaged."

"You think so?"

"Definitely, and if you're convicted of these sex crimes, you're going to be behind bars for at least thirty years, and when you're inside, the other prisoners are going to make it hell for you."

"That's what Tyler said."

"Your kid is right. I know you don't want to hear this, but your wife was stabbed to death, which is a lot better than being shot. Believe it or not, the maximum sentence for that is fifteen years. That's a lot less than for child pornography, which is five years per count. Plus, you'd have to register as a sex offender for the rest of your life. No matter where you go, whenever you move somewhere, you'd have to register, and, uh, you're going to be hounded."

He dropped his head into his hands. "How is this happening?"

I patted his shoulder. "I know this is crazy, but right now, you have to put aside all the craziness and think about the consequences and options without emotion. The rest of your life is at stake."

"I'm screwed either way."

"You've got options. They may not be what you want, but if you're honest with yourself, one is way better than the other."

"I can't believe I'm even thinking about doing this. The whole thing is crazy. I mean, I beat the murder rap."

"I know, but you understand how confessing is better for you in the end?"

"Yeah, I hear you, I hear you. I got to talk to my lawyer about it."

"If you want, I know the best criminal lawyer in all of Florida. He's handled a bunch of murder cases. I can talk to him about all this."

"That would be great, man."

"No problem. It'll be interesting to see what he says."

"I'm against confessing, but it can't hurt to hear what he has to say."

I WAITED UNTIL NOON BEFORE GOING TO SEE CRANE.

There were about a dozen protesters gathered in the street in front of his house.

Keeping my head down, I sent a text to Crane and walked briskly to the door.

Crane cracked it open, "Come in. What's going on?"

I slipped inside. "I thought it'd be better to talk about this in person."

"About what?"

"I just got off the phone with Joe Bruno, the criminal lawyer I told you about."

"Bruno? Yeah, I heard of him."

"You should've, he got that deal for the woman who shot her husband's girlfriend dead."

"Oh, right. She got a short sentence if I remember."

"She did. I tell you, Bruno is the best."

"What did he say about my situation?"

"He felt it would be easy to cut a deal. He remembered the murder and said since it was still unsolved and fourteen years old, the prosecutors would be hungry for a solve. It would make them look good, you know, that they didn't give up. It would give them a chance to make points with the community."

"Okay, but what about any jail time?"

"Bruno said a deal for ten years would be a good result and one he could get."

"Ten years? Oh man, that's a long time."

"On the surface it is, but I know him and trust him. So, I ran the child porn charges by him."

"What did he say?"

"That you were looking at a minimum of twenty years. He said they rarely made deals in child porn cases, and when they did, the defendant had to agree to chemical castration to cut the jail time down."

He threw his hands up, "Chemical castration? Screw that shit, I'd never do that."

"Bruno said Collier County is really tough on sex offenders."

"I'm not a damn sex offender! I didn't do anything. You don't know me that long, but do you think I could do something like that?"

"No. I don't. But like I said, it's not a matter of whether you did or didn't, the public thinks you're guilty."

"That's bullshit, and I'm going to fight it. I'll beat this in court, just like I beat the murder rap."

I asked to use the bathroom, and when I came back, we ping-ponged over confessing for a little while. It became obvious Crane wasn't going to confess. It was another position I hadn't anticipated. Was I losing my touch for revenge?

Pushing the doubts aside, I stood. There was a final card to play.

The task required a fresh burner phone. I drove straight to the storage unit we kept in Lee County. We were down to three new burners. I grabbed one, making a mental note to have Mario replenish the stock.

Parked in a nearby Walmart, I activated the phone. I went inside the store and bought a cheap tablet.

A young couple gave me dirty looks when I moved the car close to the entrance of the store. I powered up the new tablet and signed onto the retailer's free Wi-Fi.

Using a fake Facebook profile, I posted into four Naples groups:

Posted by The Justice Warrior

I got the below from a friend with excellent law enforcement contacts.

If you can believe it or not, it's proof that deviant Atlas Crane is still dealing in child porn. It's from a Dark Web site, they call them forums, where pedophiles hang out. Why do these places even exist?

SeXplicit4Sale: Did you check out the new drive?

CraneBuys12: Got it yesterday.

SeXplicit4Sale: How did you like the new pictures?

CraneBuys12: Even better than the first batch

SeXplicit4Sale: Good. I got plenty more coming including some unreal stuff out of Thailand

CraneBuys12: How much?

SeXplicit4Sale: Two grand.

CraneBuys12: Not a problem, let me sell some of this new stuff first.

SeXplicit4Sale: DM when ready.

Crane is a sick individual. Why did the cops release him?

We need to make sure the police find the disgusting crap that creep is hiding and put him behind bars.

Come on, Naples, make some noise about this!!! The safety of our children is at risk!!

I went back to the first group I'd posted inside of, and the comments were already rolling in.

SunAlwaysShines1962: *A Creep with a capital C!*

NaplesGal1955: *I'm about to throw up! We need to demand the police do something about this pedophile!*

The number of shares was inching up. I logged off and pulled away from the entrance, parking behind the store. Using the burner, I called the Collier County Sheriff's Office, asking for the Sex Crimes Unit.

"SCU, this is Detective Grimes."

"Uh, I want to report something."

"Your name?"

"I have to do it anonymously."

"Okay. What is it?"

"You know that man, Atlas Crane, you arrested him for child pornography?"

"Yes. What about him?"

"He's at it again. There's posts about him on Facebook in the Naples groups. Look, the posts are right. I know he got more of that porn stuff in his house."

"And how do you know this?"

"Trust me, he told me. He said he just got some new stuff. He's a very bad man."

I disconnected the call and drove away. Taking the

Immokalee Road exit, I stopped for gas at a station by the Strand. After sticking the nozzle in, I called Detective Moreno.

"Hey, Moe."

"Beck, how is it going?"

"I hear Atlas Crane is at it again."

"The phone is blowing up with calls from the public."

"I figured it would. There were a couple of posts on Facebook."

"A tip came in as well. We're going for a second search warrant."

"Really? You think you missed something?"

"We're hearing it could be something new."

"He just got out. Everybody is looking at him. He'd have to be nuts."

"No one said Crane was the sharpest knife in the drawer. Besides, these pedos can't help themselves, it's an obsession with them."

48

———————

THE PARKING LOT FOR IGOR'S BAR WAS MORE THAN HALF FULL. Was he running a special happy hour?

The hum of the place dimmed considerably when I stepped inside. All heads turned in my direction.

The place was loaded with thugs. Florida was sunny but full of shady people. The question was, were they patrons, or had Igor replenished his ranks?

I nodded to the dozen, thick-necked men leaning against the bar and strode toward the door leading to the back room. I noted the shaved-head table was back at full strength as one of them got up to intercept me.

"What do you want?"

"Igor is waiting for me."

"What do you want?"

"Tell him Beck is here."

He knocked on the door and stepped inside for a moment. The door swung open. "Go in."

Two men, with heads a bulldog would be proud of, stood on either side of Igor's desk. A bottle of vodka and several shot glasses sat on the right-hand side of the desk. The pair were new recruits. Was Igor back at full strength?

"Beck, sit. You want a drink?"

"No. I came here to talk."

Igor snapped his fingers, and the bruisers left the room.

"Did you check around for Bev?"

"Yes."

"Where is she?"

"Igor has a good idea where."

"Good idea? Nothing specific?"

"Vladimir has four, maybe five locations at most."

"And where are they?"

"All of them are in Fort Myers, with one in Cape Coral."

"What kind of places are they?"

"Bars, strip joint, you know, places we call a massage place."

He slapped the desk and roared with laughter.

"Which one is Bev at?"

"Igor get the word she goes between two places, the strip joint and the whorehouse in Fort Myers."

The words stung. Could Bev break free from such a tarnished past?

"What are their names?"

"No need for details, Igor will get her."

"Come on, you have my money. The least you can do is tell me where she is."

Igor shook his head. "Igor is handling this. You will get your girl."

"When?"

"Three days. Igor need the time for more new muscle."

"How are you going to get her from Vladimir?"

He smiled. "It will be messy but fun. Maybe you will read about it in the papers."

"Why don't you let me help? Tell me where he does business, and I can get the cops to hassle him."

"No, Igor must handle. Igor need to leave no doubt who is in control."

It was useless trying to convince Igor to tell me where Bev was. After one last attempt, I finished with, "You said you'd give me Bev in three days, right?"

"Yes."

"Okay, three days it is. I'll see you then."

I hopped in my car and drove to a gas station. But I wasn't there to fill up. I made a call. "Hey, Mario."

"Beck, how did you make out with Igor?"

"It looks like he's picked up a lot of new guys. He said he's got a bead on where Bev is."

"Great. Where is she?"

"He wouldn't say. I think he's planning something. He said he'd have her in three days."

"That's okay, I guess."

"No. It's not. I don't know what he's got up his sleeve, but it felt like he was going to try and teach Vlad a lesson, you know, make a move with a show of force."

"A good old Russian mob war?"

"I don't want to chance it. Bev will end up in the middle of it."

"What do you want to do?"

"Igor said she was working at either a Fort Myers strip joint or, uh, a brothel, run by Vlad. We need intel on where they are."

"You want to try a rescue before Igor gets there?"

"Not try. If this thing between Igor and Vlad gets nasty, I want to be sure Bev is nowhere near it."

"Let me see what I can dig up. There's like fifteen strip joints in Fort Myers, but massage places are a dime a dozen. I'll get right on it."

"If Bev is there, it's got to be one of the busier operations Vlad has. He would want her close to keep an eye on the girls."

"That's a good point, man."

"We don't have time to waste."

49

"THIS IS KATHERINE RIGBY OF WINK NEWS REPORTING LIVE from Livingston Estates."

The camera zoomed in on Atlas Crane's house. Two uniformed officers were standing in front of an open front door.

"About two hours ago, the Collier County Sheriff's Office executed a search warrant on a house belonging to Atlas Crane. This is the second search of Mr. Crane's home. Viewers may recall the initial search which led to Mr. Crane's arrest on child pornography charges.

"Mr. Crane was released on bail two days ago and was preparing for a trial. Our sources tell us an anonymous tip was received by the Sheriff's Sex Crime Unit that prompted the request for a second search.

"It's unknown what police believe might be in the house and whether they missed it during the first search or if it was recently acquired by Mr. Crane."

The reporter pointed in the direction of the cameraman, who turned around, panning a large gathering.

"The residents of this Livingston Estates neighborhood have been actively protesting since we broke this evolving story. As you can see, they're out in force again, to express the outrage they feel toward one of their neighbors.

"We spoke with a couple of neighbors before this broadcast, and a common complaint was why it was taking so long to put Mr. Crane behind bars. Some also mentioned that Atlas Crane had been put on trial for the murder of his wife, and they felt the jury had gotten it wrong by acquitting Crane of that murder charge.

"WINK News will continue to follow this important story and update you as soon as we have something to report."

I clicked off the remote as Laura came out of the bathroom. Her hair was wrapped in a towel.

"What are you watching?"

"The news. The cops are searching Atlas's house."

"Again?"

I smiled. "Yep."

She scrunched her face before unwinding the towel on her head and said, "I'm going to see Dawn. Do you want to come?"

"No, I can't, I have a couple of things to do."

"You haven't seen her in days."

"It's been hectic."

"She needs to know you care about her."

"I'm trying to find her mother, aren't I?"

"I know, but you can still make the time to—"

"How long are you going to be there?"

"I don't know, why?"

"I'll take the ride, but I need to be back here no later than one."

Dawn opened the door, putting a finger to her lips. "Abby finally fell asleep."

The apartment was as messy as it had been the last time I'd visited.

Laura said, "Did Abby sleep last night?"

She wagged her head. "It was a nightmare. She was up crying all night."

I said, "Then something is bothering her. She has to go to the doctor."

Laura smiled. "She's teething, that's all. Did you use that teething ring I got for her?"

"Oh, yeah. I forgot all about that. I'll look for it."

Laura went to the fridge. "I put it in here. The cold numbs the pain in her gums."

Dawn said, "I didn't know that."

"My mother taught me that trick when we watched my cousin's baby."

Dawn's face crumpled. "I'm doing the best I can. I had no mother or anybody to tell me what to do."

Laura put her arm around her. "We know, honey. You're doing great."

I chimed in, "You are, Dawn. Abby is perfect."

She shrugged. "It's so hard figuring out what to do. I just don't know sometimes."

There was an uncomfortable moment of silence, which I filled by saying, "It'll be easier when I find your mother. You'll see, she'll know what to do."

Dawn started crying, and Laura shook her head as she tightened her embrace of Dawn. She mouthed for me to go outside, and I sheepishly headed for the door.

I retreated to the shade of a covered parking area across the way. Laura came out waving me back.

I hustled over. "Is she okay?"

"Yes, but you have to watch what you say in front of her. You know she was abandoned."

"Look, if there's anybody who knows it's a sensitive subject, it's me. All I'm doing is trying to help."

"Well, you're not helping."

"How can you say that? I'm risking my ass and forty grand to get Bev back for her."

"Oh, really?"

"What?"

"You're doing all this for Dawn?"

"Yes."

"Come on, Beck. You're doing this for yourself. You're trying to save Bev out of guilt. But you're acting like you're a knight in shining armor running a rescue mission."

My jaw dropped. "I'm . . . No. That's not the way it is."

"It sure is."

There was too much truth in what she said. "Then how do you explain the fact I didn't start looking for Bev until I found Dawn?"

"The old wounds surfaced when you found Dawn. She looks like Bev, and then realizing she had the same last name brought all the guilt back."

Why was it satisfying to point out the obvious to someone, but it sucked when you were on the receiving end?

"That's not how it was. Besides, if it weren't for Dawn, I'd have no idea where Bev was or even if she was alive."

"Come on, I don't understand why you can't just admit to it."

"Can we just say it's a complicated situation and stop the arguing?"

"I'm not arguing. I just want—"

The ringing of my phone stopped her. If the call was spam, I was still going to answer it. I checked the screen.

"I've got to get this, it's Larson."

She turned around and I took the call.

"Hey, Ray."

"Hello, Beck. I just got word the sheriff's office is going live on X with a statement on the Crane search."

"They're doing it on social media?"

"They've had a social media coordinator for a year now. Using a social media platform gives them more reach than holding a press conference. It's a good way to combat the heat they're getting from the Facebook groups around here."

I opened up the X app, saying, "It's a time-saver not having to go. And we don't have to wait for the news to air it."

"Time is the only asset you can't replenish. Good luck."

He was right about time. It was like sleep, you couldn't make up for a lack of it.

I typed Collier County Sheriff's Office in X's search bar. A live feed had a female officer stepping up to a podium.

"My name is Katy Washburn. I'm a media relationship officer in the sheriff's office. I'd like to thank everyone here for attending as well as those watching online.

"In the last forty-eight hours, information came to the attention of the department and an anonymous call was received. The combination of the two prompted the department to seek the judicial authorization to conduct a search, which was granted."

She scanned the audience before continuing, "Earlier today, we executed a second search of the home of Atlas Crane.

"Mr. Crane was released on bail pending a trial on several counts of child pornography.

"The new search uncovered a USB drive hidden in a toilet tank as well as a kit used to prevent leaving fingerprints. The initial search included a thorough search of the bathroom, including the toilet tank.

"This leads the department to conclude the materials confiscated today were hidden during the brief period Mr. Crane has been released.

"The material on the USB is being examined to determine whether Mr. Crane may have engaged in further illegal activities.

"We'll update you as soon as we have concrete information. Thank you."

As she stepped down from the podium, the reporters in attendance shouted questions: "Is Mr. Crane being rearrested?" "What kind of information did you receive?"

The video ended. The dialogue box went black, and a replay button appeared.

50

____

I PUMPED A FIST, THANKFUL THAT SOMETHING SEEMED TO BE working. The distraction armed me with the juice needed to face Laura.

Reaching for the doorknob, my phone rang. It was Tyler.

"Hey, Tyler, how is it—"

"They searched my father's house again. The police said they found a thumb drive and something else."

"I just heard about that."

"Was it you who put it there?"

"Me? What makes you think I had anything to do with that?"

"Come on, Beck. You started all this crap."

"Hold it right there. You're the one who started this, not me. But to be fair, your old man started it by killing your mother."

"Okay, okay. I'm just worried over these sex charges. You know what they'll do to him in jail."

"All he has to do is confess and the charges will go away."

"Are you sure about that?"

"Yes. We'll make sure everyone knows he was framed. He'll probably end up getting sympathy over it."

"Why does everything have to be so complicated?"

"Life, relationships, your physical body, they're all complicated. Don't worry, the plan is going to work."

"Are you sure?"

"Absolutely.

"I can't wait for this to be over."

"Look, I've got to run. So, take a deep breath and let the plan play out."

Laura and Dawn were in the kitchen. The microwave was humming.

Whispering, I said, "Is Abby still sleeping?"

Laura said, "She's stirring and will be up soon."

Dawn headed for the bedroom. "I hear her, she's up."

I didn't hear anything.

The microwave beeped and Laura removed the bottle. She dripped some of the formula on her forearm and nodded. "Perfect temperature."

I said, "How'd you learn that?"

"My mother showed me when I had to take care of a girlfriend's baby."

"Moms know everything."

She smiled. "They do."

My phone chimed with a text as Dawn carried Abby into the room. It was Mario.

I sent a message back, asking for a call in twenty minutes.

Leaning into Laura, I whispered, "I have to get going."

Laura said, "Does she need to be changed?"

"Oh yeah."

Laura smiled. "Maybe Beck can do it."

"Get out of here. The kid is hungry. It'd take me an hour."

Laura spread a baby blanket on the table. Dawn laid Abby down and I hiked a thumb toward the door.

Laura said, "The formula is ready. We've got to take off now, Dawn. I'll see you in a day or so."

Waiting for the garage door to open, my phone rang. It was Mario.

Laura said, "You're not getting it."

I rolled into the garage. "I'll call him back."

"Isn't that why we left? So you could talk?"

Who needed AI implants when there was a woman's intuition?

"You know I have somewhere to go."

"Where?"

"Come on, Laura. I can't do this now."

She pecked my cheek. "Go ahead, call him back."

Instead of telling her I didn't need her permission, I said, "Thanks. Don't shut the door. I'll meet you inside."

"Hey, Mario. Sorry about that. What's going on?"

"I got solid information on where Bev might be."

"Where?"

"It's more than likely she's working either at the Allure Strip Club or at Oasis Massage."

"How sure are you?"

"It's rock solid."

"Where'd you get it from?"

"The Albanians. I told them we wanted to sic the cops on Vlad because he was dicking us around on a deal we made with him."

"Good thinking."

"I thought so. Now, what's the plan?"

"I'm sorry, Larson's calling. Let me take this and I'll get back to you."

"Sure, bro."

I switched calls.

"Hi, Ray."

"Hello, Beck. I just got the news. It's happening within the hour."

51

———

Hustling inside the house, Toby followed me as I put the TV on.

I opened the rear sliding door. "Come here, boy. Do your business out back. We'll take a walk later."

Ears on the TV and eyes on Toby, I watched him pick out the perfect spot to relieve himself. Finished, he bounded inside, and I gave him a treat.

Perched on the edge of the couch, I scrolled through the Naples Facebook groups. I kept refreshing the feed, but nothing was coming up.

The WINK News weatherman was droning on about the possibility of rain. The weather was nearly perfect every day, but they had to inject the chance of downpours to keep viewers tuned in.

My eyes were glazing over when a red band proclaiming breaking news rolled across the bottom of the screen. The weather map gave way to a male anchor in a cobalt-blue sports jacket.

Seated behind a console, he said, "We'll get back to the

weather after this special report. Take it from here, Katherine Rigby."

The reporter was standing in front of Crane's home.

"Thank you, Jake. I'm reporting from Livingston Estates where, just moments ago, the Collier County Sheriff's Office arrested a Naples man.

"Atlas Crane was brought under custody for what we understand are several new counts of child pornography. Mr. Crane had been out on bail awaiting trial when a second search of the residence you see behind me turned up additional evidence.

"Atlas Crane was involved in another high-profile criminal case. About fourteen years ago, Mr. Crane was put on trial for the murder of his wife, Ana. Mr. Crane was acquitted and that case remains unsolved."

My phone started pinging with Facebook notifications as the reporter said, "Our legal expert confirmed Mr. Crane will be arraigned tomorrow, and he believes the court will refuse to grant him bail."

The correspondent put a finger to her ear, pausing before saying, "We're going to go live to the sheriff's office for a statement."

A video feed of a uniformed police officer standing behind a podium filled the screen.

The policeman said, "Atlas Crane has been rearrested and is being processed at the county jail. While conducting a secondary search of his home, our officers discovered additional evidence to both support and expand the heinous charges against Crane.

"Our prosecutors will file amended charges within the next twenty-four hours. We're confident that the evidence we have will result in a conviction. Residents and visitors of Collier County can rest assured that the sheriff's office remains vigilant in protecting our community from predators and criminals. Thank you."

The blue-blazered newscaster came back on. "WINK News is proud to have brought this breaking and important story to you. We'll update you with developments as they come."

I clicked the TV off and picked up my phone. Three consecutive posts about the arrest had been accumulating comments and shares like flies to a dead frog.

Sitting back, I relaxed before tensing up. The next day or two we'd see if the Crane plan worked and whether Bev would be liberated.

Digging in my pocket, I pulled out my wallet and took the old photo of Bev out. She was a kid back then. I rubbed my thumb over her image.

I closed my eyes, trying to envision how she looked today. A wave of fear forced my eyes open.

Everyone lost their innocence as they grew into adults, but Bev had been drowning in a world of evil.

Shaking my head, I jumped to my feet. It was no time to get blue, there was work to do. Later we were going to try to rescue Bev. If we were successful, we'd deal with whatever condition we found her in.

52

———————

Inhaling slowly through my nose, I counted to four. I held it for seven seconds before exhaling for eight seconds. I realized I hadn't made the whoosh sound I'd read about and made sure to do it on the next cycle.

Sitting at a red light, I repeated the process two more times to finish the round. The light turned green, but the snakes in my stomach were still slithering.

I checked the rearview mirror. Mario was behind me. He followed me into a McDonald's parking lot and slid into a space beside me. We got out of our cars.

Mario said, "What's going on?"

"I just want to make sure how we're going to handle things."

"I told you a million times, I know what to do."

I put a hand on his shoulder. "I know you do. I'm just being cautious."

"Don't worry. We'll get Bev."

"I hope so."

"You worry too much."

"This is dangerous."

"We'll be fine."

"If you see her, text. Don't try to do anything by yourself. I need you to wait for me."

"I got it, if I see Bev, I'll message you and wait."

I opened my arms to embrace him.

Mario scrunched his forehead.

"What's going on with you, Beck?"

"Nothing. Just looking forward to everybody being together again."

"It'll be cool."

"It's been too long."

"For sure. You're going to bring her straight to rehab?"

"If she needs it. All right, let's get moving. Text me when you're there."

We pulled out of the lot. At the next intersection, I made a left and Mario turned right.

Shapely legs in stilettos stood in for the Ls in the Allure Strip Club's sign. A break in the eight-foot-high hedges surrounding the place was for the driveway. I pulled the nose of my Beemer in.

Heart pounding like the Atlantic surf, I stopped for a security guard. Unsmiling, he stared at me. I lowered my window, but he waved me through.

I scanned the lot. It mirrored a dealer of Bentleys and Ferraris. A pair of Lamborghinis were parked just off the club's main door. More than one person took a Lambo to get a lap dance?

Eyeing the two-story building, I circled the lot. I backed into the shadows of a spot with a view of an outdoor staircase leading to the second floor. A pair of black Escalades were parked by it.

Using my phone, I snapped pictures of the license plates of three high-end cars in the row in front of me. You never knew who was here and how that information might be useful in the future.

A white Range Rover pulled up and its doors popped open. Three men in their forties got out and the SUV drove away. They horsed around with each other as they went toward the entrance.

A text came in from Mario: *I'm here. Going in now.*

Be careful. If you see her, text and wait for me.

The corners of the lot were the darkest, providing the most cover. While trying to envision a quick getaway, a white Maserati pulled in.

I grabbed my sports jacket off the passenger seat and waited for the driver of the Italian sports car to get out. A man in a suit with rounded shoulders got out.

Hopping out myself, I pulled my jacket on and followed him inside. A hostess, all smiles and sequins, greeted us.

Over the pulsing music, she said, "Welcome, gentlemen, would you like a booth with table service?"

The older man said, "We're not together."

"Oh, sorry. Would either of you like to enjoy our VIP area?"

The white-haired man shook his head and brushed past her.

I said, "Maybe later."

"Remember to have fun, gentlemen."

Who was the brainiac who associated the word gentlemen with strip clubs?

Two large men, both wearing earpieces and in black, watched me as I cut to the right. Their stances screamed ex-military, and their faces, Russian.

They had clear lines of sight over the floor and stage. The music was loud and driven by the bass. Intermittent red flashes of light told me there were at least four cameras.

Three dancers, two of them twirling on poles, had the attention of the sixty or so drooling patrons. The stage was ringed in pink neon lights and littered with currency tossed by salivating males.

I hopped onto a barstool, and a bartender with less clothes than a casino cocktail waitress slid over.

She leaned over and smiled. "What can I getcha?"

It was difficult not to stare at the Grand Canyon of cleavage. "I'd love a vodka, but I'm taking antibiotics. Make it just a club soda, please."

"One little ole drink ain't gonna hurt you."

"Maybe later."

She scooped ice into a glass and stuck a nozzle in it. Placing the seltzer water on the bar, she said, "Are you new here?"

"Not exactly, it's my second time."

She smiled. "A satisfied customer."

The bartender went to serve another client, and my eyes drifted to the bank of windows for the second floor.

The stage was a distraction from the real action taking place in the upper suite of bedrooms.

Biceps bulging, a bouncer in a black T-shirt stepped into my line of vision. He swatted a customer's hand off the ass of the girl giving him a lap dance. If you wanted more, you had to take it upstairs and pay.

The formula was time-tested for centuries and played directly to the most basic of male desires: toy with a man to sexually arouse him, and then get him to pay up for the release.

I tensed and swiveled the chair back to the bar. A shaved head I'd seen at Igor's the first time I was there was leaning against the back wall.

Placing a twenty on the bar, I picked up my club soda. Keeping my back to the shiny head, I moved to a table in a dark corner.

At the next table, two men were drinking champagne and talking in Russian. Two younger men approached. They bent down and chatted for a second. Money was exchanged in a handshake. Then another clasping of hands, where a baggie was handed off. Drugs were being sold. Vlad had to be getting a piece of the proceeds, or these dealers would be floating in a canal.

I watched the buyers head for the men's room and discounted the idea of following them. If Bev was here, there was a chance she would be in the VIP area.

Heavy perfume announced the arrival of a waitress. I chatted with her, wondering if her face hurt from holding a fake smile. Despite her push, I refused a drink but tipped her twenty dollars.

I sauntered over to the VIP Section, amused by the red velvet rope and sign proclaiming a two-thousand-dollar minimum spend on beverages. The real money wasn't selling handbags to the wealthy, it was being made on vices.

The goon manning the entrance to the high-roller area gave me a look sharp enough to cut.

A flash of blue caught my eye. A woman in a short dress was climbing the stairs. My chest tightened.

It looked like Bev. I took a step forward.

It was her.

A man in a tailored suit called out to her from the bottom of the stairs. Bev turned around to respond.

I took off. Weaving through tables, I was only twenty feet away.

Bev saw me but continued up the stairs.

Screams rang out behind me. I turned. Glass shattered as Igor and a group of men burst into the club.

The music stopped.

A spray of bullets hit the ceiling. Pieces of the ceiling fell to the floor as one of Igor's men yelled, "Where's Vladimir?"

Bullets flew. I shouted, "Bev! Bev!"

I ducked behind a velvet booth. Bev disappeared up the stairs.

A sharp-dressed man bounded up the stairs two at a time. It was Vlad.

Crack! Vlad was hit by a bullet. He collapsed on the stairs.

Vlad's men returned the fire. I crawled toward an emergency exit. A body tumbled to the left of me. It was Igor. His shirt was soaked with blood.

Gunfire crisscrossed the room. The pole dancers screamed. It went dead quiet for a moment.

I poked my head up. The dancers lept off the stage, running for the stairs. Customers bounced off each other.

Another burst of gunfire. *Thud*. Shaved head's body banged into my shoulder. The hole in his face poured blood.

In a leopard-like crawl, I aimed for the red light of an exit. Pausing before crossing an exposed area, I inhaled deeply and sprinted for safety.

I burst through the door and stumbled into the parking lot. The sirens wailing in the distance were closing in. Cars jockeyed to get out of the lot.

I looked over my shoulder; two men were carrying Igor to a waiting SUV.

Crouching, I made it to my car. I grabbed my pistol out of the glove box and started the car. Following a yellow Ferrari, I turned out of the lot. The lights of police cars bounced down the street. I floored the Beemer and screeched away.

53

I PULLED INTO A PARKING LOT FOR A BAPTIST CHURCH. AFTER parking in a darkened area, I called Mario.

"Where are you?"

"In the parking lot of Oasis. Did you see Bev?"

"Yes."

"I'm coming."

"Hold on! Igor and his guys shot up the club."

"They did? Are you okay?"

"Yes. It was frigging crazy. Igor and Vlad both got hit. There were bullets flying everywhere."

"Holy shit. How many casualties do you think?"

"A half a dozen, including Vlad and Igor."

"I don't get it. Igor said he wasn't going to make a move for three days."

"He must have figured we'd try to beat him to Bev. And that worries the hell out of me."

"Why would he? I mean, you paid him forty grand."

"I don't know what he's thinking. But we were so close to getting Bev."

"Where did she go?"

I explained how the shooting began when I spotted her, and finished with, "It's a good thing she was ahead of Vlad on the stairs."

"Yeah. How bad were Igor and Vlad hit?"

"Igor had a chest wound, and Vlad, I think, took a shot in the thigh."

"You think Bev is still there? I mean the cops would detain everybody."

"She and the others probably left using the outside staircase."

"You didn't see her outside?"

"No. But a couple of SUVs by the stairs tore ass out of there."

"Shit."

"I feel terrible about this."

"Why? You tried your best."

"I don't know about that. I should've went up the stairs after her."

"Isolated on the stairs with a clear line, they would've picked you off like a wooden duck at a carnival."

"I could've crawled up the stairs and—"

"And if you made it up there, then what do you think Vlad's guys would've done? Thrown a party for you?"

"Look, you better get out of there. Once the Lee County Sherriff's Office starts looking into the shoot-up, they're going to be pawing over anything connected to Vlad."

"I'm leaving now."

I hung up and called Larson.

"Hey, Ray."

"Beck, are you okay?"

"Yes."

"I heard about what went on between the Russians and was worried you might have been caught up in it."

"It was a close call, but I'm fine."

"Are you sure?"

"Absolutely. All is well except I wasn't able to get Bev."

He paused. "You may never get her."

"I know."

"Did anyone see you up there?"

"No. Based on the cars, there were a bunch of Naples guys, but no one I recognized."

"You never know, but then again, they wouldn't want to broadcast where they were."

"That's true."

"I'm glad you're all right."

"Thanks. I wanted to keep you apprised."

"I appreciate it."

"What do you hear on Crane?"

"I talked to his lawyer. It looks like he's going to come clean tomorrow."

Toby was waiting by the door when I came in.

Laura walked into the hallway. "Did you get Bev?"

I shook my head. "No, another bad lead."

She embraced me. "I'm sorry."

"It's okay. We'll get her."

"I was worried about you."

"Why?"

"You said you were going to Fort Myers."

"And?"

"Didn't you hear what happened up there?"

"No."

"Come on, you had to know there was a big shoot-out at some nightclub."

It's a good thing I never mentioned the Russians or she'd piece this together. "I heard something on the radio but no particulars."

She pointed to the TV. "It's all over the news."

A bullet list of items WINK was covering in the next segment included the shoot-out and Crane's arrest.

"I'll watch it after I eat. I'm starving."

"There's turkey meatballs and pasta in the fridge. Is that good?"

"Perfect."

"Go wash up, I'll heat it up."

After drying my hands, I pulled out my phone and sent a text to Detective Moreno:

Need to talk. Breakfast tomorrow?
Sure.
I'll see you at EJ's in Bayfront at 8.
See you then.

The air was tinged with salt as I walked along the sidewalk fronting the marina. A boat was motoring away from the dock. Moreno parked across from EJ's and I hustled over.

"Good morning, Moe."

"Morning, Beck." He pointed to the cloudless sky. "It's another good one, ain't it?"

"Sure is."

We sat at a table in the rear. A server filled our cups with coffee and took our orders.

"What did you hear about what happened in Fort Myers last night?"

He raised an eyebrow. "You had something to do with that?"

"I'm just a guy hanging out at a titty bar."

"You were there?"

"As an observer only. I got a lead on Bev, but all hell broke out before I had a chance to do anything."

"Geez, Beck. You know these Russians think life is cheap. You can't be—"

"What did you hear about Igor and Vlad? They got shot."

"They're in Lee Memorial Hospital. Igor is critical, and Vladimir along with three others are in serious condition."

"Any of the victims female?"

"I'm not sure. Why? You think one could be Bev?"

"I doubt it."

We silently drank our coffee. The server delivered our breakfast.

I dabbed my sunny-side up eggs with toast and Moreno ate a piece of bacon.

I said, "Didn't you get the memo on bacon?"

"If I can't eat what I want to, what's the point of living?"

"Eating stuff like that might shorten the time you're on the planet."

He picked up another piece and smiled.

I lowered my voice. "I need something."

"What?"

I told him what I wanted.

He put down the strip of bacon without taking a bite. "That's risky."

"So is eating bacon."

"All right. Let me see what I can do."

I slid a Publix bag holding a new burner phone across the table. "This is fresh. I loaded a new number on it just for this."

54

I kept checking the burner I was using for Moreno. Nothing.

"Toby!" I jingled his leash. "Let's go for a walk."

We left the house and walked to the end of the street. Toby lifted a leg on the stop sign's pole.

The burner pinged. A text had come in. I opened it.

"Come on, boy. Let's go home."

We hurried inside. I grabbed a treat, tossed it to Toby, and went into the den. I closed the door and opened the message. It was tough to read on the burner, but sending it to my laptop or another device would leave a trail.

I expanded the picture of the document. It was on the Collier County Sheriff's letterhead and read,

I, Atlas Robert Crane, confess to the murder of Ana Margaret Crane in the early hours of June 1st, 2011. Early that morning I went to 9943 Hunters Road in Naples where I used to live with my wife and son.

I had gone there to talk to my ex-wife about getting back together. I was upset she had been seeing someone and hoped we could fix things up.

Ana wouldn't answer the door, so I had to use the code to the garage door to get in.

She started yelling at me as soon as I came in the house. She told me to leave and began cursing at me. I tried to talk to her but she was really angry and kept arguing with me.

I tried to calm her down, but she just wouldn't.

All of a sudden, she grabbed a knife out of the block of knives on the kitchen counter and threatened me with it. I was scared. I knew I had to take the knife away from her, but before I had a chance to do anything, she attacked me.

In the struggle to get the knife away from Ana, she got stabbed. I panicked and ran instead of calling for help. I didn't think she was hurt as bad as it ended up being. If I knew, I would've called 911.

The guilt over her death has haunted me for fourteen years. I'm telling you this now because I'm innocent of the child pornography charges against me. Those files on my computer aren't mine—they were planted by someone to destroy me because of what I did to Ana.

Coming clean after all these years about her death shows I'm not the monster the press and my neighbors think I am. I killed Ana in a fit of jealous rage, but I'm not a pedophile and have never been involved with or even looked at child pornography.

This confession was made freely and voluntarily without any threats or coercion.

It was signed, *Atlas Robert Crane*

Below his signature were the signed attestations of two witnesses who confirmed that the confession was given voluntarily and that Atlas Robert Crane understood the contents of his confession.

Toby pawed at the door. It was unusual for him. I got up and opened it. I hadn't unhooked his leash.

I did and he scampered off. I closed the door and sat back down.

Reading the confession again, blood started pulsing in my ears. Crane was shifting blame to his wife for starting the confrontation. It was outrageous.

He'd gone there in the middle of the night.

Crane was forty pounds heavier and eight inches taller than his wife.

I pounded a fist on the desk. There was no struggle. She had multiple stab wounds in the chest area. She wasn't stabbed by accident. He stabbed her to death and fled. The only thing he was sorry about was being forced to confess.

I took the photo of the confession and posted it into three Naples Facebook groups. Navigating back to Naples Vibe, the first group I'd posted in, brought a smile to my lips.

The comments and shares were going up faster than the numbers on a gas pump.

DolphinDebbie1964: *I knew he did it. That POS should rot in jail.*

TurtlesRule: *Good job Naples PD!*

NYCEscapee: *Jail is too good for Crane. Shoot him or hang him in public like the old days.*

It was only a matter of time before the sheriff's office issued a statement on the confession.

The usual high never lasted when I finished a job, but with this one, I didn't get a boost of any kind. I wondered if it was because my mind was on Bev.

I called to let Larson know the confession had been made and then reached out to set up a meeting with Tyler.

Before I got out of my car I checked X, and there it was. The sheriff had posted a statement on the Crane confession. I read it quickly, focusing on the last sentence:

There was no evidence to support Mr. Crane's assertion that he was being framed with the child pornography charges.

Tyler was sitting on the same bench off Seagate Drive where we'd first met. A family of ducks was motoring around the edge of the bay.

My gaze settled on the duffel bag by Tyler's feet.

"Hey, Tyler."

"When are you going to get the porn charges dropped?"

"Is that my money?"

He picked up the bag and handed it off.

I unzipped the bag. Tyler said, "It's all there."

"I'm sure it is."

"So, what about the porn stuff?"

I zipped the duffel up and said, "Meet me tomorrow at the Coastland Mall. Inside by the food court."

"What time?"

I said, "Noon." And walked away with the cash.

55

IGOR WAS STILL IN INTENSIVE CARE, BUT VLAD HAD BEEN upgraded to stable. The other injured were recovering, with two of them being released today. The shoot-out was in the news, but because no one had died, the story was fading.

Wherever Bev was, I hoped she and the rest of Vlad's gang were lying low. There was no doubt Vlad's people would be looking for retribution for the ambush.

Closing my eyes, I pictured Bev on the stairs before the shooting began. She didn't appear to be using drugs, or at least nothing strong. She looked good, but when our eyes met, her face was a mask, not the foster sister I remembered.

I was waiting for a call from Mario. I'd sent him to see Dren the Albanian, hoping he'd have information on the fallout. Would he come back with a lead on where Bev was?

The Coastland Mall's food court was buzzing with the chatter of snowbirds and teenagers being teenagers. Much of the talk was in Spanish.

The smell of burgers and fries wafted through the air.

Tyler was sitting at a table by the Chick-fil-A store. Walking by the Japanese Sarku place, Tyler jumped to his feet and rushed me, saying, "You said you'd fix it. It's a mess."

A gray-haired couple turn their heads toward us.

I hissed, "Keep it down, kid."

"Come on, I paid you a ton of money and—"

I grabbed his wrist and twisted it, leading him to the last table in the area. "Sit and keep your voice down."

He frowned and sat.

I dragged a chair next to him and sat. "You paid to get justice on your father. He's behind bars for killing your mother, and not getting out any time soon, just like you asked."

"But the porn charges, you said you'd get them to go away if he confessed."

"I changed my mind. Your father is a lowlife who deserves what is coming his way."

"You can't do that. I'll go to the police and tell them what you did—"

I drove a knuckle into his thigh.

"You open your mouth, and you'll go down with your old man."

"What are you talking about? I didn't do anything."

"You planted the porn on his phone and laptop. Remember the fishing contest?"

He hesitated before saying, "Yeah. What about it?"

"I had cameras set up below deck. We have you on video uploading it onto your father's phone."

"That's bullshit!"

I leaned in. "Keep it down."

He put his head in his hands. "I can't believe this."

"Believe it. Your father is a coward and a killer. Don't feel sorry for him. He's where he belongs."

"But . . ."

"No buts. He murdered your mother, and then has the balls to blame her? I heard he made himself a deal with the confession. He'll be out in something like fifteen years. I'm sorry, Tyler, but that's just not good enough."

"He's not a good man, but this seems like it went too far."

Squeezing his shoulder, I said, "He deserves everything he's getting. Your mother didn't get a chance to see what an incredible son she raised."

He shrugged.

I said, "You were deprived of your mother, the most important person on the planet, because of him. Plus, don't forget he misled you for years."

"I still miss Mom."

We were aligned on the hole that losing a mother created. "Do you understand why we had to do what we did?"

He nodded. "I get it."

"Good. It'll feel better as time passes."

"And I'm going to stick to not visiting him or writing to him."

"You're a smart kid."

He smiled.

My phone buzzed. It was Mario. I stood. "I have to run, but I'll keep in touch."

"Okay. Thanks for everything."

We shook hands. I looked him in the eye and felt he wouldn't change his mind about things. But I'd tell Mario to go see him to make sure he'd abandoned the idea of getting the porn charges dropped.

Hustling to the exit, I answered the call. "Hey, Mario. How did you make out?"

"Better than expected."

"What did the Albanian say?"

"I think being happy about the Russians fighting with each other made his lips looser."

"Get to it, bro."

"Okay, okay. So, Igor is in worse shape than it seems. He's still in intensive care."

"It's good to hear the information I'm paying for is accurate."

"You still using Pedro at the hospital?"

"Yes. What else?"

"Vlad's planning an attack on Igor's gang. Dren said they're looking to take advantage of the fact that Igor is out of commission. He thinks it's going to be a major war. Vlad is pissed Igor had the balls to attack him like he did."

"That makes sense."

"It does, but Igor's guys are making noise about going after Vlad."

"Igor's injured worse than Vlad, so a response is in order."

"Exactly, they want to put a hurt on Vlad."

"Did he say anything about Bev?"

"Not specifically, but he heard Vlad is moving his key people out of harm's way."

"Where are they going?"

"He said they might be going somewhere in the Keys."

"The Keys?"

"That's what he said. Vlad has that big-ass boat, and they could be using it to ferry them."

"Where in the Keys?"

"He didn't say."

"See if you can find out. When is this supposed to happen?"

"I got the feeling it could be tonight."

"Vlad's boat is at that tiny marina on Bay Street?"

"Yeah, that's right. It's right where Lucky Strike Fishing Charter keeps its boats."

56

I HUNG UP THE PHONE AND TOSSED IT ON THE COUCH.

Laura said, "Larson hasn't heard anything on Bev?"

"Nope. I'm putting the grill on."

"It's not even six yet."

I didn't want to tell her I was trying to get my mind off Bev.

"I'm hungry—besides, my stomach doesn't know what time it is."

I put the grill on and took tuna steaks out of the fridge. After running them under the faucet, I basted them with oil and spices.

"Do you want green beans with it?"

Laura said, "Okay, but slice up some tomatoes too."

"Yes, ma'am."

I took the beans out, and the burner in my pocket buzzed. It was my contact at the Lee County hospital.

Stepping out to the lanai, I answered, "Pedro. What's going on?"

"Vladimir checked himself out."

"What? Are you sure?"

"Yeah. A couple of his guys came. He discharged himself and left."

"When?"

"Just now."

"Okay. Thanks."

I came back inside. "Laura, I have to run."

"Now?"

I opened the door to the garage, using my leg to keep Toby inside. "Yeah."

"Call me."

Racing south on Route 41, I slowed down. A Naples Police Department car was at the red light on Harbor Drive. I'd never forgive myself if I missed Bev because I'd gotten pulled over.

It was tougher keeping to the speed limit after the turn when Route 41 headed east. The road was wide and empty, but I kept it under sixty.

I made a right onto Bayshore Drive, slowing down for a car who couldn't decide whether to turn into Celebration Park or not. Tapping my horn, the car pulled into the lot.

Where was the turn for Santo Domingo Drive? Was it this far down? Spotting it, I slowed and pulled onto Santo Domingo Drive. Turning onto Nevis Way, I snaked my way around to Bay Street.

I decided to park in the lot for an industrial building housing a boat maintenance business. I got out and surveyed the area. It was quiet.

The marina ahead only had a dozen slips. Vlad's boat was one of six docked there. At least three of them bore the signs of the Lucky Strike Fishing Charter outfit, and another was a small speedboat parked next to the Russian's craft.

I crossed the street, working my way to a peninsula which was home to Wakeboard Naples. Across a small body of water, it provided a clear line of sight to observe the comings and goings.

It was me and the mosquitoes until a white Mini Cooper drove to the end of Bay Ave. The driver parked on the grass across from the homes lining one side of the street.

I moved out of the sight of the gangling man in a T-shirt and shorts as he walked along the boardwalk to the tiny marina. I couldn't see him but heard his footsteps.

I poked my head around the edge of the hexagonal building and saw him step onto a boat. It was Vlad's yacht.

Darkness was closing in, and the man put the interior lights on. He fiddled with something in the rear of the boat. I smacked the back of my neck crushing a mosquito. Looking at my blood-smeared fingers, the running lights on Vlad's boat came on.

It was a sign the boat would be leaving. The man on the boat sat on the bridge and checked his watch. Five minutes later, he started the boat. He was the captain.

As the engine rumbled, I crouched down, moving to the other side of the building. Standing behind a rack of paddleboards, a white SUV came into view.

I squinted as the passenger and back doors opened. Three men and a woman got out and headed toward the dock. The SUV made a U-turn and took off as its passengers hit the boardwalk.

One of the men was limping. It was Vlad. The woman was wearing a hoodie. She was the same height and build as Bev, but her face wasn't visible.

Inside my head, I pleaded, *Come on! Look this way.*

Cars doors slammed. My head swiveled toward the lot where I'd parked. Four men were running to the boardwalk. They had guns.

Vlad and his crew looked over their shoulders and started running. The woman's hoodie fell onto her shoulders.

It was Bev.

I reached for the gun strapped to my ankle as the captain of Vlad's boat threw off the lines and shouted in Russian. He ducked below and came up with a machine gun.

Standing on the dock, he sprayed bullets in the direction of Igor's men. They retreated, taking cover. The captain reached his hand out for Vlad.

Vlad had one foot on the boat when the captain took a bullet to the shoulder and fell into the water.

Vlad shouted in Russian. Bev and the men followed him past his yacht. The two men fired shots before jumping into the speedboat. They helped Vlad get in.

It was now or never. I stepped out. "Bev! It's me, Beck! Jump in the water. I'll get you."

Bev looked in my direction and leapt.

She landed in the speedboat. One of the men tugged at the cord to start the engine.

Igor's men were sprinting toward them. The speedboat's motor roared to life and pulled out of the slip, fishtailing as it headed for safe waters.

Bev was gone, again.

I hid behind a rack of life jackets as Igor's men took off. After they got into their cars, I held my hands up and approached the captain, who was trying to stay afloat.

I hoisted him onto the dock and checked his wound. After calling 911, I left.

57

———————

I HANDED THE KEYS TO MY BEEMER TO THE VALET AND HELPED the girls out of the car.

"Welcome to La Playa, sir. May I help direct you?"

"We're going to the beach. Our friend, Ray Larson, is a member here."

He pointed. "Excellent. Mr. Larson is in the front row, to the right. Just follow the path and enjoy your day."

"Thanks."

We made our way to the beach, lugging all the extras needed with a baby in tow.

Larson wore a smile and a bathing suit with penguins on it. "I had them put out four chairs and three umbrellas. Is that good?"

"Perfect, Ray. This is nice. You finally broke down and became a member."

He pecked Laura's cheek and went straight to Dawn, who was holding Abby. "Oh my. What a cutie this one is."

Ray made stupid faces and sounds that adults made for babies. He turned to Dawn. "There's plenty of shade on the end. If you think it's too hot for her, we'll get a quiet spot inside."

"Thank you. It's so nice here. I haven't been to the beach since before Abby was born."

"I'm glad you came. Oh, if anybody is hungry, there are menus on the chairs. Order whatever you like."

The girls carried Abby to the Gulf and put her feet in the water.

Settled onto a chaise next to Larson, I pointed. "I wish I remembered my first time at the beach."

"Most people were simply too young."

"Hey, thanks again for inviting us."

"Anytime, Beck. You know that."

"I do, and I appreciate it."

"Usually I have to twist your arm to get you to do anything."

"I needed a break, we all did."

"You have to take care of yourself and your relationships or nothing matters."

"That's what's driving me to get Bev."

He hesitated for a long time before saying, "I received some information on her."

I bolted upright. "What? Where is she?"

"I'm working on that, but Vlad was seen in Miami. The early word is they left the Keys."

"Miami? I guess it makes sense."

"It seems he wanted to recover completely, and the information is, he did."

"Where in Miami? Is Bev with him?"

"I'm working on it. This is not the time or place to get into it."

"But—"

"It's early, as soon as I have something, you'll know. Now relax, enjoy yourself."

"How can I relax after you told me that?"

"You have to learn to compartmentalize. Something always needs doing, somebody is always hurting, etc., etc. Learn to live in the present moment and you'll be happy."

It was something I needed a lot of work on. "It's easier said than done."

He motioned toward the water. "Leave the fight for another day and enjoy what we do have."

I got off the chair and stripped off my Nirvana T-shirt. "I haven't been in the Gulf in years."

DID YOU ENJOY THIS ISN'T OVER?

PLEASE RECOMMEND IT & REVIEW IT

THIS ISN'T OVER

The exciting third book in the Art of Payback Thriller series

THERE IS MORE TO COME IN THE ART OF PAYBACK SERIES.

STAY UP TO DATE!

FOLLOW DAN PETROSINI AT WWW.AMAZON.COM/AUTHOR/DANPETROSINI

WHILE YOU WAIT FOR THE NEXT BOOK IN THIS SERIES HAVE YOU READ, THE LUCA

MYSTERIES?

Vanished: A Luca Mystery Crime Thriller: Book #1

The Luca Mystery Series

Am I the Killer

Vanished

The Serenity Murder

Third Chances

A Cold, Hard Case

Cop or Killer?

Silencing Salter

A Killer Missteps

Uncertain Stakes

The Grandpa Killer

Dangerous Revenge

Where Are They

Buried at the Lake

The Preserve Killer

No One is Safe

Murder, Money and Mayhem

The Golden Sellout

Suspenseful Secrets

Cory's Dilemma

Cory's Flight

Cory's Shift

Art Of Payback

Race To Revenge

Beyond Revenge

This Isn't Over

ABOUT THE AUTHOR

Dan is a USA Today and Amazon best-selling author who wrote his first story at the age of ten and enjoys telling a story or joke.

Dan gets his story ideas by exploring the question; What if?

In almost every situation he finds himself in, Dan explores what if this or that happened? What if this person died or did something unusual or illegal?

Dan's non-stop mind spin provides him with plenty of material to weave into interesting stories.

A fan of books and films that have twists and are difficult to predict, Dan crafts his stories to prevent readers from guessing correctly. He writes every day, forcing the words out when necessary and has written over twenty-five novels to date.

It's not a matter of wanting to write, Dan simply has to.

Dan passionately believes people can realize their dreams if they focus and act, and he encourages just that.

His favorite saying is – "The price of discipline is always less than the cost of regret"

Dan reminds people to get the negativity out of their lives. He believes it is contagious and advises people to steer clear of negative people. He knows having a true, positive mind set makes it feel like life is rigged in your favor. When he gets off base, he tells himself, 'You can't have a good day with a bad attitude.'

Married with two daughters and a needy Maltese, Dan lives in Southwest Florida. A New York native, Dan has taught at local colleges, writes novels, and plays tenor saxophone in several jazz bands. He also drinks way too much wine and never, ever takes himself too seriously.

He puts out a twice-a-month newsletter featuring articles, his writing and special deals and steals.

Sign up at www.danpetrosini.com